THE MAZE OF IMMORTALITY

AARUNI AKKI

Made with ♥ on the Notion Press Platform
www.notionpress.com

For my caring parents and beloved sister who always
believed in me.

Contents

Contents

Contents

Foreword

Dear Readers,

To say that I am biased would be an understatement, but I assure you that my admiration is not at all familial loyalty—it is genuine awe.

From the moment I read the first page of this book, I was transported. The words danced across the paper, weaving a flow of emotions, memories, and dreams. Each chapter revealed a piece of the author's soul, a glimpse into their innermost thoughts.

This book is more than a collection of sentences and paragraphs; it is a mirror reflecting our shared experiences, our shared humanity. It invites you to laugh, to cry, and to question. It whispers secrets and shouts truths.

So, dear reader, I'm telling you: immerse yourself in these pages. Let the prose wash over you like a gentle tide. Allow the characters to become your confidantes, the plot twists your companions.

To my sibling: You have poured your uttermost efforts into this work. May it touch the lives of many, just as it has touched mine.

With love and anticipation,

Avani Akki

Preface

A little girl is willing to take on a journey to find her long lost parents. No matter the challenges, she continues to thrive, willing to do anything to reunite with her family. She soon finds herself in a world where magic exists and lands in a maze. She runs through each challenge, and finally faces the one who had caused her pain and the one who had separated her from her family...

Acknowledgements

As I reflect on the completion of this book, I am overwhelmed with gratitude for the many people who contributed to its creation. Writing this story has been an amazing journey, one that I could never have undertaken without the help and encouragement of so many.

First and foremost, I would like to thank my wonderful family. To my Mom, Mangala and Dad,Veeresh, your unwavering belief in me and your never-ending support throughout this process have meant the world to me. Thank you for always being there to cheer me and for instilling in me the confidence to pursue my dreams. I am eternally grateful for your guidance and love.

To my dear sister,Avani, thank you for being my constant companion on this adventure. Your enthusiasm for my writing and your willingness to listen to my ideas and stories have been invaluable. Your belief in me has been a source of strength and inspiration, and I am so lucky to have you by my side.

I would also like to thank my uncle Amarnath Akki who has been instrumental in editing and bringing out this book elegantly in an extremely short time.

Finally, to all the readers who pick up this book, thank you from the bottom of my heart. It is my greatest hope that my words will bring you joy, laughter and perhaps even a little bit of inspiration.Thank you for giving my story a chance.

Prologue

Adeline heard something and turned around, her eyes wide open at her sight. 'What do I do?', Adeline said to herself. The shark approached closer swimming so fast, in seconds it was right next to Adeline. She thought and without hesitation, balled her fist and lunged at its gills. The shark felt nothing but instead planted its sharp teeth into Adeline's shoulder. Adeline screamed of terror and shut her eyes close. She couldn't hold her breath for so long... couldn't get back up, couldn't move at all. She couldn't hold the pain as blood dripped from her shoulder where the shark had bit her.
She needed help, desperately...

1

Adeline woke up and was startled when she checked the time it was 8;45 AM, she was late for school, it was a sunny Thursday morning. Her parents were already at work they always left home at 5:30 AM and Adeline had to depend on her alarm clock but with her little sister, Annie who would always mess with it, it was way harder than it seemed. Annie was awfully smart though and so was Adeline but she always had problems with being early to school. She was in 7th grade and she was going to become 12 in 2 months. Adeline was scared of so much stuff, such as heights, confined places, and spiders.

Other strange things happened in her life for example whenever she was determined to know something she would just feel something in her mind and she would be able to read people's thoughts that she could see.

And whenever she felt angry, she seemed to control someone else or even the weather but that happened only for about a minute.

One day when she was on the bus to school, something really strange happened...

A stranger with blue eyes looked at her and seemed to be trying to control her as her hand wanted to move in weird ways until she felt so angry that she put her hands up and a fire formed in her hand but it was a blue one then she threw it to the man with full force and the man disappeared.

But the people around her didn't notice anything so she just tried to believe that it was a dream but part of her knew that it was not, and what happened there was real. since that day she would always feel weird and feel like she had powers but whenever she tried to explain to her parents the situation, they would not believe her.

She slid off the bed, brushed her teeth, bathed, changed her clothes, and went to the kitchen she took some milk from the fridge and cereal but unluckily some of the cereal spilt. She quickly cleaned that and started eating while combing her hair. She realized she had missed the bus so she had to walk to school.

She sprinted as fast as she could and when she finally reached the school she was panting and sweating. She stopped outside to catch her breath. She tiptoed into class and slid into her seat which was right next to Jenny's, her one and only friend in the whole school and life. She sighed; the teacher's back was facing her.

Unfortunately, not many people talked to her and no one liked her so the most popular girl said out loud, 'Oh look, Adeline's late once more. She should be expelled! Who's on my side?' Adeline was so angry and she gritted her teeth. That girl's only goal was to make people's life as miserable as possible.

As soon as Ella had said that, the professor turned and looked at me, clearly looking frustrated. I tried to hide in my seat, but it made no difference. The professor said, 'Adeline, I'm very disappointed in you. You come late every single day and you never change. Well, I don't know what else to do but give you one whole week of detention and play at lunchtime, don't even think about it, you're going to have to sit alone in this class and eat your food silently. Now, don't waste your, mine and all the other students' time and take out all your things. Give me your homework!' Finally, after 45 minutes of work which felt like an eternity, the bell rang and all the children left their classes.

Jenny started one of her big lectures on chess and Adeline felt drowsy ready to sleep. The weight on her eyes was too much.

Adeline was walking home from the school. She was exhausted. The streets of the city were as busy as usual and Adeline squeezed through the big crowd of people. She hated people and always hated being the center of attraction.

Adeline hid her face and rushed to an almost empty street. It becomes really hard to search for an empty street in New York. 'Woof', a bulldog barked. Adeline eyes opened and she ran for her life she wanted anything it wasn't to be chased by a bulldog in an empty street and get bitten with no people to help around.

One thing about Adeline was that she was so afraid of dogs. Long story it's also one of those stories which contained magic in it.

When Adeline was 5 years old, she was in a park, her parents were talking to their friends and Adeline had ventured far away from the park. She was chasing a beautiful butterfly. At that time, she used to love dogs. After a few minutes, she saw a dog, but this one was not like the other dogs she used to see.

This dog was really strong and dangerous. No messing with it or else you die. A strange man was walking it. Something about the man just made 5-year-old Adeline's skin crawl, Adeline couldn't see the man's face. He wore sunglasses and behind them, Adeline thought she could see red eyes that were shining brightly.

He wore a golden bracelet on his wrist. Adeline ran away and hid behind a tree. She peeped from behind it and saw a boy aged around 14 approached the dog and man. The boy went to pet the dog but as soon as he touched it the dog charged for the boy and tore him apart. Adeline covered her eyes.

The man snapped his fingers and the dog and the man disappeared taking the boy with them leaving no trace. Adeline rushed back to her parents. But she didn't tell her parents a thing.

Back to reality, out of the blue, she saw a girl appear from thin air. Adeline's jaw dropped and she was so surprised. 'What the hell is happening!' She thought to herself. As soon as the girl had appeared, the dog suddenly vanished and she was so shocked she just stood there frozen and opened her mouth like a goldfish and immediately closed it.

'Now, now I know you're very confused but listen, you just need to trust me. It's a long story and I'll explain it to you as soon as we get back to where you belong.'

Adeline felt an instant sense of regret coming into this empty street and she was so confused and so scared.

Adeline was a coward then. She took all the courage she had and said, 'How could I trust a girl who appeared out of thin air and made a dog disappear? Give me a good reason.' The girl raised her eyebrow and muttered a few words and then took a deep sigh and said, 'Well if I were a danger to you, I would have already done something. This is an empty street so, it's not like anyone would see you so why would I be wasting my time.'

'Oh well, fine. I hope this is worth it.', Adeline muttered.

'Oh, trust me I am taking you to a place which compared to

this place looks like it's almost heaven. It's the closest thing to heaven. You'll see once we get there.'

'Wait a second, one day, I was in a park and saw someone terrifying wearing the same bracelet as you. How could I possibly trust you? Get away from me!', and with that Adeline was going to run away but the girl just gripped her hand so tightly that she couldn't even dream of getting out of her grasp.

'They're different. I'll show you something to prove you can trust me. And as soon as we go, you must tell me every single detail about this man you told me about.'

The girl was about to show her something when they were interrupted by a violent shake. It was an earthquake and a very terrible one. 'Adeline, follow me!', the girl said shouting to be heard. The buildings were collapsing and breaking into pieces. People were running around the streets crying for help and screaming.

Adeline ran and followed the girl as she was her only hope. Soon, she caught up with her. Suddenly, a building was about to crash into Adeline but luckily, the girl pulled her away at the perfect time. 'I hope that was enough to prove to you that you can trust me!', the girl shouted and Adeline shouted back, 'Totally!'

Soon, they arrived at a dead end. There was a big brick wall. 'Don't worry, I know what to do.' She kept her finger on a brick and enchanted some words. Then to Adeline's shock, a door appeared. They pushed it open. As soon as they entered, the girl closed the door and enchanted a spell once more. 'Just keep hold of that chain right there okay? Don't let go of it.', the girl said. Adeline did exactly what she said.

As soon as she touched it, it felt like she was as light as a feather. As she had acrophobia, she didn't dare open her eyes afraid that she was going to see herself in the sky and the land as small as an ant.

She was surprised she was still holding the shining object. She counted her breaths, and when she reached 37, she landed with a thud but it didn't pain as she thought it would, there was something incredibly soft where she landed. She finally opened her eyes and looked up to see the girl who had rescued her coming down towards her at a very fast pace. Adeline got out of the way and stood firm. She looked around and saw many people but she realized something was odd. They were all wearing a strange bracelet around their right wrist it was almost the same bracelet she had seen glowing when she had teleported here and it took a moment for her to realize that she was wearing a bracelet similar to the one that that strange girl was wearing.

Millions of questions flooded her mind and she wanted to get the answer to every single one of them how did she teleport here? -is this whole thing a dream? -does magic exist and can I do magic? Etc...

As soon as the girl had landed and got up Adeline asked, 'What's your name?'

'Avery, I'll explain everything to you. Well follow me, this spot is not too safe, you can expect someone to just slide down and fall on you and that will cause a lot of injuries.

2

"Where are we?"

'we're in Slopindon the best place for dwarves, I see how confused you are just follow me. I've been looking at you for the last two years and I also did look after you at home, you see I acted like your neighbor. To transform into someone's you need a special potion with that takes a week to brew and I don't recommend it, it tastes like vomit but a little sugar on it and juice mixed with it and mushed pizza it also is really weird when transforming into someone's body and you need some ingredients that I cannot mention that's classified as only the highly-qualified knows about it I am not a part of them but I tend to help them for some little tasks here and there. We dwarves are green and our world is full of colors and we don't like looking old so there is another tasteless option that makes you look young. We also have a long lifespan of around 1000 years and death and violence is rare. we also have schools here it's really fun. I wonder how humans can even handle sitting there listening to how to do calculations!"

Dwarves didn't look the way humans described them. Most of the dwarves looked pretty young after drinking the potion that Avery had told them. And they were interested in plants. The place was surrounded with trees and they were not regular trees some trees had golden apples hanging from them. Avery followed Adeline's gaze, snatched an apple and said, 'These apples are special. Take them in your hand and think of a food and when you bite the apple it will taste like the food you were thinking of' she gave Adeline the apple. She thought of a pizza slice with extra cheese, black olives, green pepper and tomatoes and when she bit the apple it tasted just like she thought it would she gobbled the apple in a few seconds, that was the coolest thing ever. There were so many plants but most of them were not green.

Adeline followed Avery to a beautiful mountain which was very tall, it had snow all over its peak. "But I don't see anything here is this really where the highly qualified and the president or whatever is , I mean on a snowy mountain? And do we have to hike till there that would take days this mountain is almost as tall as Mount Everest. Ok that might be a slight exaggeration but still, I don't want to die, I'm still very young."

'No, we don't have to hike till there, that's pathetic. I just advise you to hold my hands tight, close your eyes, and don't panic'

Before she could ask any questions Avery took her hand and held tight. Adeline kept her eyes close and tightened her grip on Avery. She felt the same feeling she had felt when she had taken the glowing chain and teleported to Slopindon.

But this was slightly different, this time it was way faster and she didn't feel so panicked as she knew that something strange was going to happen. When Avery said that she could open her eyes she did as she said and she was stunned. The place had glass crystals as decoration, the floor was solid gold, there were beautiful paintings on the walls; made from more glass crystals, chandeliers were hanging from the roof and there were 8 different people seated on chairs made from blue diamonds and a very comfy cushion. One of them said, 'Hi my name is Natalie, I see that Avery got you here I will be answering all your questions and you will be answering some of my questions. Aveline has the power to see if people are telling the truth or lying so we are going to see if you are honest to us and don't hesitate to ask your questions.

We will escort you to a room and take some time to adjust to this – you have magic powers that can save the world, but you'll have to train and besides you're a child, that's not your job. Luckily, we don't need to save this world Slopindon is safe, for now.

You are unique and have many powers to make you believe this remember in the bus when you threw a fireball at the person who was controlling you that's rare, with that power you can conjure fires whenever you become angry and it is hard to control, the more the angrier the bigger and stronger the flame. In school, you will be taught how to improve your skills in same time controlling them and you have way more abilities to discover I understand it's really hard to swallow this information, so we will leave you for a few minutes in your room to think of this – from now you will be living in Slopindon and you will be taken care by some people. They're super sweet.'

3

Natalie escorted Adeline to a room that was like a royal guest room it had a bed with a fluffy, velvet blanket, puffy pillows and a mattress so comfy Adeline almost fell asleep when she lay on it. The bed was bigger than two queen-sized beds joined together, there was a closet full of snacks there was a compartment for sweet items with-skittles, chocolates, Ferrero Rocher, Candy Floss, and lollipops. In the sour section there was stuff Adeline had no idea existed then in the spicy and salty section were her favorite snacks-Doritos, Pringles, lays, bingo, Cheetos, and Takis, her mouth watered by its sight. there were also 5 bookshelves full of books, a closet for clothes, a modern table and a chair.

Natalie said,' You will be staying here for three days until we find somebody to look after you. I hope you like this place, all meals will be served on that table"

"But what about my family, won't I get to go there?"

"Unfortunately, you won't for now, we are doing this for your safety, alright, it's not safe there now. We have brought all your belongings here and I know you might be thinking why can't your family come here, it's because they can't live here, the air is different here and they would get issues breathing if they would come here."

After a few minutes, Natalie and Aveline returned and she

answered all the questions they asked and vice versa. After, they gave her a slip of paper with the schedule for the school that she would be attending. Most of the best people in Slopindon went to that school Adeline checked her timetable and realized she would be spending 7 hours at high peaks. On the first day, the teacher would just put the student's skills to the test. And then they would be grouped into categories depending on their powers and levels.

The timetable was:
Monday
Tuesday
Wednesday
Thursday
Friday
Survival
Concentrating
potions
History
swimming
snack
snack
snack
snack
snack
history
survival
potions
survival
music
sports
controlling

sports
Controlling power
survival
potions
potions
survival
concentrating
potions
lunch
lunch
lunch
lunch
lunch
controlling
Mind reading
Figure out abilities.
Mind reading
history

The school was starting tomorrow and she was optimistic. She started with snacks, followed up by a delicious dinner, and later had dessert: a slice of cheesecake and an Oreo milkshake.

After that, Avery peeked her head and came in. 'I'm here to answer all the questions you have, well not all. You'll have to sleep after some time because school is starting for you soon. Hit me with all your questions.'

'So, tell me was that dog chasing me your fault?'

'Yes. But that dog was fake and even if you wanted to, you wouldn't be able to get harmed from it, I wanted to lure you to that specific place so I sent a dog to chase you till there.'

'Well, I don't have many questions because Rosaline and

Aveline already answered all the other ones so the only question is do you go to High Peaks?'
'In fact yes'
She later went to bed, and as soon as her head hit her pillow, she fell asleep. The next day, she did her toilet and put on her uniform; a blue cape which was not necessary so Adeline decided to keep it in her school bag which Natalie had prepared for her, a blue pants with two small pockets in which she could barely fit her handkerchief in, a white shirt with the logo of high peaks; 2 mountains covered in snow put on the top left of the shirt. She did her hair in a loose low ponytail locked her room and left. Natalie said she would teleport with her, she also said that the first week they wouldn't be following the timetable.

It was a ginormous school with 14 floors and a garden bigger than her school in her old life. There was a fountain in the middle and in front of that, an assembly was being held.

The principal was saying, 'Good morning, everybody, we are starting a new year at our school. As you all know we have new students here too. first of all, we have Della Froster in grade 7...'The principal continued with all the new people's names until she announced Adeline's name and they all started clapping, Adeline went red. She never liked being the center of attraction. When it was over, she followed the grade 7 kids and someone came to talk to her.

you're
She said, "Hi my name's Melanie the new person in class, aren't you?"
'Yes', as soon as Adeline thought she had a friend Melanie said, "Well you must know, you'll sit alone on your table for lunch that is if you even get one"
Melanie's friend busted out laughing and left Adeline

angry, very angry! The class was staring at her. Adeline was confused, why was everyone staring at her? Adeline took her two hands up and a flame erupted in them she covered one hand on the fire then threw it at the floor and shouted in her mind, then she breathed in to calm herself and water came in her palms she poured it on the fire and both of them disappeared when Adeline snapped her fingers. Adeline was shocked. The whole class was surprised; this had made her some friends. A group of four came to her and all of them just said, "Wow"
Adeline replied with a gentle smile, " I had no idea I could do this I thought I had only one power though, well I need to go to class, Bye!"

4

She rushed to the class accidentally bumping with someone who said 'You're the one who conjured fire and wiped it out with water and then made the water disappear in a snap of your finger and you're new I'm surprised. My name is Sophie Carter and I'm in grade 8 I'm ashamed to say that your powers are way better than mine people usually only have one or two but I bet you have at least 4 right and why I was ashamed I am the top of the class not to brag and you're going to get late to class if you don't run and if professor Brielle is teaching you then you're dead. she scolds you even if you're a minute late I'd rather skip her lessons. They are so boring. She speaks in the same tone just like a robot. Nice to meet you though bye."

And with that, Adeline ran to the class. Luckily, Professor Brielle was not teaching her and she was just 3 minutes late she went in the class. In this session, they would be testing their abilities while kind of fighting with the other members of the class but in this class the years 7,8 and 9 would be together so the class was bigger than some others it had benches but no tables. There were hooks to hang the bags too.

Adeline had shown her powers in the morning when she got angry so nobody wanted to go fighting with her which made Adeline proud. The professor set Adeline with a boy who turned out to have mind reading and how to control water and make someone hurt.

The different groups were set into different rooms when the professor said go the fight started. Adeline was against a grade 9 person so she was scared if he was good with his powers.

Adeline took all her anger out of her and remembered all the moments she was angry and she pictured flames and red. Then she lashed it all out creating a huge fire which she threw at the boy. But he deflected it easily. Adeline thought of binding him in ropes and suddenly a rope appeared in her hands she thought of a chair and it came in front of her. She threw the ropes around the boy and tied him to the chair then he screamed and said, "How can't I read your mind it seems like I just can't explain it. How did you even make a chair appear that's so weird you have 3 powers!"

'Actually, no I don't have only 3 I have 4 one to control water and then one to control fire, one to think of something and it appears in front of me, and one to make things disappear with a snap of my fingers. To think about it I wonder if I can read your mind."

She closed her eyes and concentrated on the brain then she plunged into it and she heard his thoughts could you have 4 powers I just have 2, UNFAIR! -but can you read my mind-I still don't get how your mind can't be read. Adeline opened her eyes and collapsed

she heard voices, most of them she didn't recognize-they were saying-she'll be waking up soon-what happened to her did Jason do anything to her.

Adeline opened her eyes and she realized she was in the nurse's office she had just collapsed the whole class was

dismissed and they were in the nurse's office a voice which must have been Jason said, 'See I.did.nothing.she's alive though she looks pale I wonder why?"
"Adeline?, Adeline?" said an unfamiliar coming from someone who she thought was the nurse.
'To be honest I don't know-I-I-wait a minute let me remember what happened'
She traced what had happened then she remembered. 'I remember-Adeline closed her eyes and then said- I had not been able to get out of Jason's mind I was trapped in there like I was one of his thoughts I travelled deeper into the mind and then reached a place where there were flames they hurt me I cried it was not affecting my skin it was affecting my mind I felt like a needle was piercing in my mind it pained so much I collapsed and that's all I remember"
Everybody looked confused and Jason looked like he was going to collapse when he whispered while looking at the ground, 'I know what happened I had been so angry that Adeline had tied me to a chair I tried to make her hurt but I didn't know that it would hurt so bad.'
Adeline was angry she had started a flame in her hand she then caught the blanket on fire then she breathed in and then conjured water to remove it then she held it longer and clapped her hands when the wind dried all the water leaving no trace. When the nurse and the professor gave her a death glare she mumbled, 'I'm sorry, I don't know how to control my powers yet. Wait did I just unlock a new power'
They nodded and Adeline froze she now had 5 powers.

5

She got out of bed and rushed out and when she saw Melanie laughing at her she made her hand into fists and punched Melanie in her stomach. She howled and started crying. Now it was Adeline's time to laugh the whole class laughed too but Melanie's friends looked like they wanted to laugh but they didn't.

'Nice job, Adeline. Wanna be friends? My name's Jolie. I will sit with you at lunch there will be 4 people there and all of them hate Melanie we wanted to do something like this to her and you did it instead. You're so cool and I won't forget you have 5 powers and they're so cool too.', said Jolie.

'I didn't know you would get hurt but I never thought that it would hurt people who come in my brain to search things. It's so cool how you have 5 powers it's unfair. I know now you have millions of people wanting to be friends with you.', Jason apologized.

The bell chimed and all the students rushed down. Adeline also needed time to rest after the throbbing feeling she had felt when she had tried to read Jason's mind.

Adeline went to Jolie and her group which had 6 people involving Jolie and Adeline. There were and all of them hated Melanie and spent a lot of time trying to prank her.

She followed them to the cafeteria where there were snacks. Adeline took some French fries and they sat on a table. They introduced themselves their names were Lily, Veda, Zelda, Jenny, Jolie, and Adeline.

She finished the fries and they went early to the next session which would be about making their powers better which would be 2 and a half hours. She went to sit on the benches and when the teacher entered, she granted them with a sweet smile. The professor made them show their abilities and then the professor would help them improve.

This lesson was a little boring as it was for 2 1/2 hours. After that, they went to lunch. In the cafeteria, there was some bread salad and cheese, rice beans and apples and other combinations. They planned how they would sneak into Melanie's house and make it rain on her without her knowing and they decided they would make her get distracted by throwing a ball at her window and then doing the trick on her. Adeline did not want to be part of it so they made somebody else do it.

Suddenly, the principal's voice said, 'Adeline, please come to my office. We need to talk." Adeline was panicking. She walked to the office with trembling feet. When she arrived there the principal looked pretty chill and Adeline felt a little better. 'Please take a seat', the principal said pointing to a seat. 'I heard that there has been a lot of stuff going on and everything includes you in it, please explain. I'm not scolding you, it's just to solve your problems.' After a few minutes, Adeline exited the office with a smile on her face, it wasn't bad after all.

There was one more lesson which was another boring lesson and then she finally teleported to her home which would be a home for 1 more day. Natalie said that there was a family she might be adopted by they just had to sign papers and then Adeline would be living with them. When Adeline went to her room she cried on her bed, would she ever see her human family ever again she was afraid to think of it. What were they thinking about her now? She decided to sleep a little so she wouldn't get angry and set something on fire.

She expected to sleep as soon as she hit her head on the pillow but she just couldn't sleep. She could hear voices outside whispering about something.

She decided to read some books and then dinner came she then could sleep as the voices had stopped. But she still wondered what they were talking about. They seemed worried but Adeline hadn't paid too much attention.

6

She teleported to the school with Natalie. She went to the line for grade 7. The assembly was about to start. The assembly was just so boring Adeline wanted to sleep. She then headed to the next class. The next class would be about concentrating. Adeline sat down on a bench and in this class, there were only 8 people sorted into 2 groups boys vs girls. There were 4 people in each group.

The professor said they would be playing a game. First 1 person from each group would be protecting a flag that person would be called the protector. If the other team captures their flag they lose. The other three were going to try to tag the other people who were on the other team they were called taggers. When someone catches you, you are out of the game. And if everyone gets caught in a group, they lose.

You were also allowed to use any of your powers. The professor walked them to the garden where there were two flags one red-girls team and one blue-boys team. The person protecting the flag for the girl's team would be a girl called Bianca she was tall and also really fast. The person protecting the flag in the boys' team was a boy called Willy one of the persons who hated Melanie. They would get 5 minutes to plan their plan.

So, Jasmine would be catching the taggers. Adeline would

be distracting the protector away from the flag while Viviana would take the flag. Bianca also was a person who controlled fire so in the beginning, she would cover the flag with fire about 100 cm tall. And then she would help Jasmine catch the taggers.

And if someone screamed now, they would circle a tagger and catch them and when that was done they would shoot fire at the protector to distract him and then one of them would capture the flag.

They stationed themselves in their spots and when the professor blew his whistle the game started. Jasmine went to tag the taggers. Adeline thought of a chair and a rope she took the rope and swung it on one of the taggers and then pulled the tagger toward the chair she set the tagger there and tagged him. Now there would be two more taggers left and it would be easier for Jasmine and Bianca.

Adeline thought of 5 Paper balls in her hands and then it came true. She hit the protector in the head and after a few tries, he got distracted and came to Adeline to tag her. Adeline ran far away from the flag and unfortunately got caught but in the meantime, Viviana was going to capture the flag. Adeline saw a tagger catching Viviana. Adeline became angry. She screamed, 'NOW!'

Jasmine and Bianca cornered a tagger. And they got closer faster and tagged him. Bianca threw some fireballs and then at the correct time when the protector's hair caught on fire, Jasmine captured the flag. VICTORY FOR THE GIRLS coach screamed. The boys looked agitated.

The rest of the class was just tagged. After a few minutes of tag and a lot of sweat, the bell chimed all the students rushed to the cafeteria. Adeline took some samosas.

When she was going to a table a girl said, 'Hi, my name's Caliana. It's nice to meet you. We'll know a lot about each other later. My parents are going to be looking after you. I've always wanted a younger sister so it will be exciting. I also have a brother we're twins. I'm in grade 9 by the way and I know you're in grade 7, though with those special abilities, you should be in grade 8, see you later.'
She waved and went back to a table with her friends. This life would be pretty weird, in her human life she had only a smaller sister who couldn't do magic, and the same for her parents. But now she would have parents and 2 siblings having powers. She wondered if they would be kind. She went to the table with the group. She spent time with them and she went back to join her classes.
The next class was mind-reading. There were only 6 people. 3 girls and 3 boys the professor was already there when all the students were there. The professor said that they would be doing an activity. They would be communicating with each other mentally. Their classes for mind-reading would always be with the same people so they would have to know each other and they would have to do that by communicating in their brains.
Adeline closed her eyes and focused on the person on her right, she sent a message. It felt like there was a pipe

connecting the two and she just had to create a thought and push it to the other person's mind. The message was-
Hi my name is Adeline what about yours when is your birthday mine is on the 16th of February and I was born in 2012, I used to live with humans. And now I have come here it will take me at least a month to get used to here.
When she opened her eyes, she saw the girl focusing and trying to send her a message but she wasn't able to. After a few seconds, she opened her eyes and said 'I am not able to send Adeline a message she sent me one easily it's hard to send her a message I even tried to read her mind but I wasn't able to. I felt like there was a thick wall blocking me from her mind. By the way, my name is Alia and my birthday is on the 24th of August I was born in 2012.'
The professor sighed, 'Adeline is unique she has an impenetrable mind. She also has many abilities. I take it she discovered 5 of them but she has more than that. Her abilities are also some of the rarest ones. One of them is controlling fire the other controlling water the other thinking of something and it comes into your hand another one reading people's minds and with a snap of her finger the thing she wants to disappear disappears. Well instead of doing this exercise, each one of you will try to pass a message to me. Concentrate. we'll do it 1 by 1. Adeline you first.'
Adeline closed her eyes and pictured the professor's face then she finally got connected to her mind. She felt a connection with her. She sent a message to the professor I am Adeline.
She then opened her eyes and saw the professor trying to send her a message. But when she opened her eyes and said, 'It's true I can't read your mind or send any messages to you. But I think with a lot of trust with some people they

will be able to read your mind and send messages.' Adeline felt worried whoever she trusted would be able to read her mind but that just felt weird.

8

Imagine having someone poke around in your brain. There were more lessons and finally, the bell rang she went to the cafeteria, and Caliana told she could sit with her at a table to talk and introduce themselves so Adeline accepted the request. She went to sit with Caliana at a table with 2 chairs. They took some bread, cheese, salad a bottle of water and a little piece of cake.

'I wanted to introduce myself and get to know you more we're going to be siblings after all. My name is Caliana Carter. I'm in grade 9. I was born on 1st of April 2010 and I don't like my birthday being on the 1st of April as my brother always pranks me. Our family loves to joke it's almost like a tradition and being born on the 1st of April is also fun as I can make pranks but I would rather have my birthday on the 2nd of April. My brother's name is called Madson Carter. He's the funniest in the family and his name suits him, he's mad.'

Adeline laughed and then she said, 'My name is Adeline Midson and I was born on the 16th of February 2012 I love reading, sketching, playing, and writing stories. I am wondering how it will feel to have a family with powers. It's still so confusing, no one can read my mind or send me any messages and I have 5 powers and very rare ones too. I wish I hadn't taken that gold chain my life wouldn't be so

mysterious'
'And your life wouldn't be this fun and safe. I heard from Avery that humans had so less colours in their lives and their world is so polluted and not safe at all and there are so many deaths. Our world is so safe the last time we had a fight was about 9,000 years ago when a group of villains not known to Slopindon came to attack us. They had many people on their side, they were very powerful and many dwarves died then about 150 of them died that was the dark days. But now we make sure we are ready to face them stronger than we were before. There are many books about that. I have 3 of them if you want you could always borrow them. Well look at that I still have my food left we better stop talking and eat.'
So, lunch passed like that in an awkward silence. Then finally the bell rang. She had many lessons one for fire controlling another for water controlling and one for fighting though Adeline wondered why they were teaching that as Caliana had said Slopindon was very safe. And the last attack happened 9,000 years ago. Adeline was pretty good at it. When the bell chimed she headed down to the fountain where Natalie stood she took her hand and they teleported home. Natalie said, 'Alden Carter and Allina Carter are offering to look after you they have twin children in grade 9 who go to the same school as you, and knowing them I know that they talked to you. Well, all you have to do is say if you're okay.'
Adeline said, 'Yes' as soon as Natalie finished her sentence. She went to pack her clothes, her pink flamingo plushie she always slept with, her accessories, and other things she packed them in luggage, and when she was done Natalie and Adeline teleported to Carter's house it had 4 floors. The house was white and there was a big garden there were

many trees and a fountain. She rang the bell and Caliana opened the gates and beamed a smile, ' I expected you guys would come soon' She was standing with her mother and they looked so similar. They had blonde hair reaching their waist, they had teal eyes and they were tall.
Allina took Adeline to the house and said, ' I heard that you and Caliana have been talking a little at school and she said you have 5 powers and the rarest ones she also said that you have an impenetrable mind I that true?'-Adeline nodded. 'Adeline Midson it's a pleasure having you as a daughter Caliana will give you a tour around the house and I will take all your items from the luggage and keep them in your room. Oh! Look at that you have a plushie too Caliana can't sleep without her blue whale and Madson can't sleep without his red dragon well that's one similarity.'
Caliana's face turned red. She took Adeline to the inside of the house the living room had a Sofa and a glass table in front then a big TV. There was also crystal decoration in the corners of the room. There were paintings of sceneries better than the Mona Lisa or the starry nights.
There was the kitchen and the bathroom as big as what used to be Adeline's bedroom. Then upstairs were two bedrooms one for Caliana and the other one for Madson. Caliana's bedroom had a bed as big as two queen-sized beds joined together there was a mirror and some jewellery. There were bookshelves with books. Caliana said, 'I am ready to give you any books at any time'.
Then on the bed was a fluffy white blanket and some pillows and there was the blue whale plushie.
Madson's bedroom had a bed as big as Caliana's and had a red dragon plushie and the same pillows and blankets. Madson was there and when he saw Caliana and Adeline

he said 'Hi, Adeline this is my room I see you finally came, Caliana was waiting near the gate for 10 minutes. Our family loves jokes too. I hope you enjoy yourself, make yourself home as this is now your home too.'
'Mom created the best joke on 1st April 2010 a few minutes after my birth and guess what it was it was you.'
Adeline had to bite her tongue to hold back her laughter. Then they went upstairs there was a master bedroom the bed was as big as 3 queen-sized beds together this was the parents' bedroom there were 4 pillows and a big, fluffy blanket there were 2 mirrors 2 wardrobes, and a bathroom. There were big bookshelves. Then they went to the last floor where there would be Adeline's bedroom. Allina had already kept all the stuff in her bedroom the only thing left to do was keep her clothes. The bed was as big as Caliana's and Madson's the pink flamingo plushie was in the middle of the two pillows and there was a pink fluffy blanket. There was a mirror and all of Adeline's jewelry. There were bookshelves and some books in them. Clearly, the family loved reading there were bookshelves in every bedroom, one more similarity. A dream catcher was hanging on the door and underneath the bed there was a white, fluffy carpet. There was another bathroom and it had gold walls and a bathtub, a sink, a toilet and all was made of gold, Adeline's toothpaste and toothbrush were there too.
'Do you like the house? Caliana asked. 'I love it. And I see your family loves reading.' Sophie said. 'Yes, we do. Do you want help for sorting out your clothes?' 'Sure! Thanks!'
Thirty minutes passed and they were done.
Caliana, Adeline, and Madson decided to play the Capture the Flag game. They invited one of Madson's friends called, Elijah. They played rock paper scissors and whoever won would decide their team first and whoever was left would

be the other person's team. Caliana won.

Caliana immediately took Adeline in her team. They planned that Sophie would tag the protector and Caliana would tag the tagger. Caliana would be the one to protect the flag she would cover the flag with fires as tall as 100 flames.

Elijah was going to be the protector and Madson would be the tagger. When Caliana said go the game started, Caliana surrounded the flag with fire. Adeline ran to the bushes and crept behind them when she thought she was behind the flag she got out. But unluckily Elijah had heard Adeline walking behind the bushes and he hurled a fireball at her when she tried to run away. The fireball hit Adeline's palm and it had a burn her skin turned purple.

She fell on her knees and covered her palm with a cloth. Then a tear ran down her cheek. She stood up and her palm Shaked she went in the house. When Caliana, Madson, and Elijah realized what happened they rushed to Adeline. One of them is called Allina and Alden.

Caliana told Adeline to rest on the couch. Allina and Alden finally came. Allina had some potions in her hands, she rushed to Adeline and poured some of them on Adeline's palm.

After a few seconds, the wound healed and it looked like nothing had happened.

9

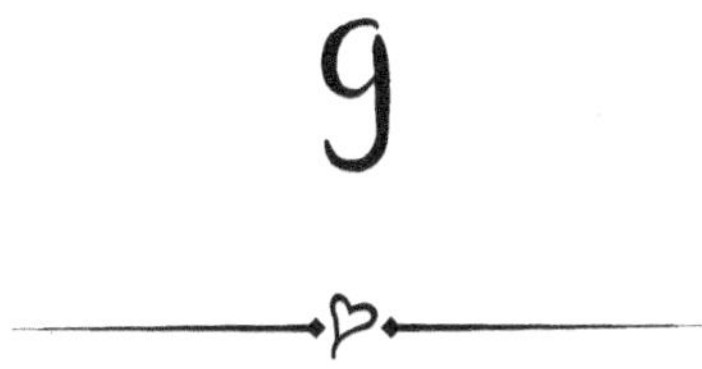

'Adeline are you all right, does it hurt anymore?', Alden asked. Adeline said, 'No, it doesn't it feels like nothing has happened.' Alden and Allina went back to do their work and Calliana, Madson, Adeline, and Elijah continued to play.

When it was time for dinner, Elijah left. The dinner was really tasty. There was dessert too. The desert was a marshmallow-looking thing that when it goes in your mouth it melts and explodes into different flavors.

That day was pretty fun. Alden and Aliana introduced themselves. They worked with the government. Adeline wanted to ask what were the government whispering about but she decided not to.

Adeline went to her bedroom brushed her teeth and went to Caliana's bedroom and knocked on the door. A voice said, 'Come in'

When Adeline entered, she saw Adeline reading a book. Adeline said, 'Sorry to interrupt. I just wanted some books about the attack that happened 9000 years ago. I have nothing to do so I just wanted some of those books and some other books about the history of Slopindon.'

'It's all right, I don't have many books about the history of Slopindon, only 1. Though my father has many books about that, I have 3 books about what happened 9000

years ago.'
Caliana went to her bookshelves took three books and set them on the bed. 'Here they are. I'll give you books about the history of Slopindon tomorrow. You can take all three of these. My favorite one of them is, 'the death of our people- 9000 years ago. The title is not interesting though. But it's my favorite one, though I don't like books about violence in Slopindon. As I said Slopindon is safe and to have people attack us and we are unarmed is just- you know- weird. That was one of the only attacks on Slopindon. There are way more places out there for Dwarves and other creatures such as elves, goblins, gnomes, and more. My father has many books about the history of Slopindon so I'll borrow some from him and give them to you tomorrow. If you want any other books tell me, I'm sure someone in my family will have it'
Adeline thanked Caliana and took the three books. She put them on the table so it wouldn't get mixed with the other books. She started to read the book Caliana had told was the best book out of the three.
She learned some interesting facts, then after a few minutes, she yawned. She put the book back on the table and went to sleep. The next day she woke up to the sound of her alarm clock. She got up and stretched her arms to get all the laziness out of her, she went to the window and pulled the drapes and looked out of the window. A little far away was a waterfall. The scenery looked so peaceful, the sounds of birds chirping and the leaves rustling. She made her bed then went to the bathroom and brushed her teeth, bathed and changed into her clothes. Today there would be P.E. so they had a different outfit. There was a white T-shirt with sleeves reaching her elbow, an optional cerulean-colored jacket, white socks reaching the knees,

black shoes and a cerulean-colored skirt. She dressed in the clothes and then combed her hair. She went downstairs. Caliana and Madson came a minute after her they were wearing a red short and skirt, white shirt, red cape, black shoes, and white socks. Adeline took Caliana's hand and Caliana took Madson's hand then they teleported to the garden of the High Peaks, the school. They separated; Adeline went to the grade 7 line. The assembly was boring as usual.

Then they headed to the next session which was the history of dwarves. Adeline went to the classroom; it had desks and chairs; this was the only classroom with desks and chairs. Adeline went to the desk in the 2nd row and but her bag on the side of her she took out her books, pens, rulers and highlighters. The class was more boring than the assembly. Turns out a dwarf called Densey Kelter had fought 9000 years ago and a bunch of more facts that were useless.

Then there was snack time she wasn't able to go with the 'we hate Melanie' group as they had gotten detention for 3 weeks as the professors had figured out who had been pranking Melanie.

Two girls came by, the girl on the right had brown hair, Brown eyes, and freckles. The girl on the left had blonde hair and blue eyes. She said, 'Hi I'm Felicia and she is Bianca. I saw you have nobody to sit with you can come sit with us. I also heard Bianca saying you guys have met and also, she seems like she's a little jealous of you. I think everyone is; I mean who wouldn't want 5 of the rarest powers.'

'I am not jealous' said Bianca a little too quickly it made it more obvious that she was jealous. Adeline smiled and said, 'I don't think she is, and I will accept your offer I'll sit with you guys. I'll brink my snack and come back to this table'

They sat down and Adeline went to take a snack, there was candy floss, Cake, Samosas, French Fries with ketchup, and ice cream. Adeline took a blue candy floss and she went to the table where Bianca and Felicia were sitting.

Adeline introduced herself and when they reached the part about powers, Adeline had a lot to share. The bell rang, and now it would be P.E. P.E. would Be situated in the garden.

They ran to the garden. The professor was there. The professor started with some stretching exercises. Then they played the game with taggers and protectors. The game was interesting as there were 4 groups; 6 people in each group. The day was fun when the school finished, Adeline, Caliana and Madson met near the fountain which was situated in the garden.

They held each other's hand and teleported home. When they reached home, Alden and Allina asked how the day was. Then Adeline went to her room, bathed, and changed her clothes. She then went to Caliana's room as she had told Adeline she would give her some books about the history of Slopindon. She took the books and started reading one.

She read until dinner; Alina called them downstairs for dinner there were tacos and ice cream for dessert Adeline munched on the food and when she was done, they talked about how the school day was. Then she went to bed she took the flamingo between her arms and slept.

10

'Hi everyone. Hope you're all doing well. Today I wanted to talk about the latest attack. As all of us know our world is safe and violence and attacks are really rare. 9000 years ago, Slopindon was attacked but we were attacked by not only dwarves but vampires, goblins, ogres, and a Cerberus. Since then, we have been learning how to fight at school since grade 5 when you're 9 or 10.

Some people got poisoned and they got transported to a maze well at least we think so we wouldn't have known about it if Walter Cane a very good fighter barely survived. He came here, he was treated in the hospital but the wounds were too big and deep so he couldn't make it he said, 'poisoned, captured, transported, maze, monsters, escape' then he died. We have been investing about it but so far, we have no idea who they were.' said Mrs Brielle in her robotic voice.

The session was another boring session. Adeline tried her best not to look at her because she had come late to class. Then there was snack time she sat with Felicia and Bianca. She headed to the next class, fighting, she was good at it last time because she had fought with a mannequin. She was given the option between a sword and a shield or a bow and arrow. She chose a sword and a shield. This time they wouldn't be fighting with mannequins, but they would be fighting with what they called dwarf hologram. It acted like a regular dwarf which won't kill you but they will injure you if you don't fight with them continuously, you need to press a button when you're done fighting and it will turn back to a statue, it also uses powers that you could choose.

But Adeline called them dwarf robots. She got paired with a dwarf hologram which looked so real, she had brown eyes, black hair, a black shirt, white jeans, and black shoes. Her powers were: controlling water, controlling electricity, and inflicting pain. The class had 18 people and they would be fighting one by one.

Sophie watched 3 people fight then it was her turn, she breathed in and stepped forward. The professor pressed a button and the fight started. Adeline held her shield up and rushed forward.

She took her sword and was about to hit the dwarf but the dwarf snapped its finger and a shot of electricity went through her she screamed, 'Ahhh!' But she didn't give up. She took her shield to cover what she was doing so the dwarf wouldn't see her and block her with water. Adeline retreated and made a ball of fire in her hands she fed it with all her angry times and then it got almost as big as her hand she came closer to the dwarf and immediately hit her with the fireball before she could do anything.

The dwarf got injured but she didn't die. She inflicted pain on her but Adeline conjured a wall when she thought of it and that lost the dwarf's focus. Then she took a deep breath and held it then a gust of wind came she snapped her finger and the wall disappeared.

Then she hurled the wind to the dwarf which made her fall, Adeline took her sword and stabbed it on the dwarf. She had killed her! The holograms didn't die they just disappeared.

The professor congratulated her and the rest of the class spent her time looking at the others fight their Dwarf Holograms. Then she had a class where only she and the professor would be there. She would be figuring out if she had other abilities.

The professor made her feel all different emotions and when he made her become anxious a bolt of lightning came into her hand and she calmed herself down and it disappeared. Then when he made her feel scared an icicle came out of nowhere.

Well, that lesson was useful. Now she had 7 very unusual powers. Most of the dwarves only had 1-3 powers and she had 4 more than that. It made her feel like an odd one out.

People sometimes called her 'the unusual one with 5 powers' now they would start calling her 'the unusual one with 7 powers.

The professor had also said with great powers come great responsibilities and that made her nervous but she calmed herself down so she wouldn't conjure a bolt of lightning. Then it was lunchtime, she went to Felicia and Bianca this time they were giving a special meal that consisted of some macaroons, pasta, coke, cake, salad, and some French fries. Adeline took that and then started munching on her food while talking to Bianca and Felicia.

11

It was Saturday and there was no school she woke up and looked out of the window. The scenery looked as beautiful as usual. She went to do her toilet and then went downstairs. She saw Alina and Alden sitting at the table eating breakfast.

When Alina saw Adeline she said, 'I didn't expect you to wake up so early, Madson and Caliana could sleep all day if I don't wake them up. It's nice not having them for 1 hour, they joke around a little too much, especially on their birthday, it's also April Fool's day so, so they prank each other

Adeline smiled and went to the table to talk with them she said, 'The day before yesterday, at school I had a class to figure out what other abilities I have, turns out I can make icicles pop out of nowhere and I can conjure bolts of lightning, now I'll be called the unusual girl with 7 powers. I always feel like I'm the odd one out why can't I be like the others, why can't I be normal why do people try controlling me on the bus?'

Alden sighed and said, 'You are normal Adeline and what others say doesn't change does it? No. I used to have the same problem when I was in 4th grade, I hadn't even gotten an ability people used to call me the useless one and I didn't listen to them it encouraged me to get a new ability.

And then I got some of the rarest abilities, like controlling people, fire, and conjuring something that I think of.'
Adeline shrugged. Then she heard a yawn she followed the sound and looked at the stairs, Caliana was coming from her room, she had black circles under her eyes. She said, 'Good morning, I decided to wake up early but I couldn't get out of my laziness and sleepiness as I had slept late reading a book. But it was worth it. I finally reached the interesting part of the book. So, Adeline's an Early bird? Well, that means I won't be able to prank her in the morning of April Fool's so sad!'
They ate breakfast which Adeline chose to be simple cereal with milk.
She and Caliana decided to play Monopoly and turns out Caliana was good at it. In the middle of the game when it was almost 10:00 AM Madson woke up and peeked through Caliana's window and said, 'Oh look at that Caliana woke up earlier than me and she's playing money polly without me.
Can I join?'
The game was even more hard for Adeline to win now. The twins always won and it made Adeline a little jealous.
The whole day passed and at night they sat on a cushion with popcorn and watched a movie. There were jump scares that made Adeline's skin crawl.
She went to bed and this night she needed her flamingo plushie way more than ever. She had millions of nightmares of ghosts. One of the nightmares had spiders as big as Adeline's hand.
That night she couldn't sleep well at all. She was glad when the first light came. She checked the time, 6:20 AM. She went downstairs to see if Alina and Alden were there, they were.

She went to talk to them and at the same time ate her breakfast. They had fun with some jokes too. But Adeline couldn't stop thinking of her nightmares.

Adeline was early for the class, there were only 3 people; Adeline, Felicia, and Bianca. They were early because after all it was Mrs Brielle who was going to teach them and she would scold them if she was a minute late. This time she came 15 minutes early. It was 7:45, she started talking with Bianca and Felicia.

It was now 7:50. The windows opened and black cloaked people arrived out of it their hoods hid their faces. Adeline let out a scream but no voice came out. She wanted to run but she just stared at the 4 cloaked figures arrive. Then one of them took a handkerchief and put it under Adeline's nose.

She was being drugged! That was the last thing she remembered. She woke up surprised to see herself in a grassy place the walls were high and made from grass. It took her a moment to realize that she was in a maze. There were 8 bows, a set of arrows, swords, and shields.

That was not a good sign. Luckily, she wasn't alone there were some people on the ground, and she recognized some of them; Caliana, Madson, Elijah, Felicia, and Bianca. There were 2 more people. One boy looked like Bianca but just bigger and one girl looked like Elijah but bigger. They all woke up after 2 minutes and when they saw where they were they looked as confused as Adeline was when she had woken up in the grassy maze.

She said, 'I think we're in a maze and there are bows, arrows, shields, and swords and all of us know that is not a good sign. I think that what happened 9000 years ago is happening again, there are more people than just us eight in this maze, and we need to escape and try to save others well if we stay alive, that is. We need to stick together too, especially at night. I wish this were just a nightmare.'

They all looked angry, confused, sad, and mostly scared.

Adeline asked the name of Elijah's sister and Bianca's brother. Their names were; Evelyn and Gerald. They took a few minutes to take in the information. Adeline looked worried and that was because she was, what if she died! She then suddenly made an icicle pop out in front of her then an idea popped into her mind, if she could make an icicle pop near the wall and make it in the shape of stairs, she could climb it and look the way out of there.

Alas! She couldn't control where the icicle popped or the shape of the icicle. She took a deep breath in then a deep breath out. Then she said, 'I think we should go' They hung their arrows on their waist, the bows on their waist, and their sword on their back.

Felicia took Bianca's, Bianca took Adeline's Adeline took Evelyn's, Evelyn took Caliana's, Caliana took Madson, Madson took Gerald's and Gerald took Elijah's

They all clung to each other. Then they continued ahead. They walked straight for a few minutes then there was a three-way fork. They went right. Then after a few more minutes, there was a wooden door.

There was a lock in it, they had to find the key Adeline and her friends started searching the space. Then a scream came from Bianca, 'I found it! It was under a big rock' She rushed to the door and stuck the key in the lock then the

lock fell.
Adeline opened the door.

43

13

The room had wooden tiles and wooden walls there were 8 chairs and a long chair in front of them. On the table were buttons in front of the chairs.

Then a voice said, 'Hi my eight contestants. I love asking riddles. I see you are willing to answer them just sit down on the chair each of you will get your turn and when you are ready to answer you should just press the red button and tell your answer. So come on get seated. And there is a door there to escape this room but there is a lock to it. I will give you the key as soon as you answer my 24 riddles.'

'Are you kidding? 24 riddles!', Madson asked. Yes, said the voice. So, all of them sat on a chair. So, the first question for Caliana and don't tense. A man walked into a room and saw three doors the first one had a sign which said Home and the second one had a sign which said Library but the third door had no sign but the man knew exactly where it led to. How?'

Caliana pressed the red button immediately and said, 'Because he had just entered through that door. Next question

a man was murdered in the house a detective came to investigate and he found a note which said the 3rd of April 1st of October 5th of March 3rd of June. The suspects were Willy, Bob, Billy, Rohn, and John who was the one who

murdered the man?'
'Rohn'
'Crack the code Pot 00000000'
'potatoes'
'Well done now Adeline's turn. What has many keys but
can't open any doors?'
'a piano'
'Who are your parents?'
'I don't know'
'Wrong! Well, if any of you get 2 more wrong well let's just
say you will not leave here. Peter's parents have four sons;
Rohn, Ronald, Rex who is the fourth son
'Peter. And besides this is just so. In.Ju.Di. Curious. asking
who my parents are is just so stupid that is not a riddle! Tell
me who they are, please!'
'Now it's Felicia's turn. It starts with t it ends with t and it is
full of t what is it?'
'Teapot. Why are you ignoring Adeline's question, answer
her. I know you know you know who her parents are tell
her!'
'Solve the code.
Ta het tafrcoy.'
'Um... at...the......factory'
'An electronic store owner came to work one day and saw
that his safe was open his money was nowhere to be found.
A detective came and the owner explained that the keys to
the safe were in the same key as his car keys. The 2
employees would always use them but they would always
return them too. The detective asks what the two suspects
know about this incident. Andrew says, 'I didn't copy the
key. I wouldn't even know which one to copy' Ryan says,
'I've been working here for three years. And I haven't
entered this room yet.' Who stole the money and how do

you know?'
'It's Andrew the detective didn't tell how the thief stole the key so how would Andrew know about it'
'Now Bianca's turn. You have to escape a room there's a code. The clue is to write backward all the letters. What is the code?'
'It's settled eht lla, you should just write all the letters backward'
'You throw me out when you want to use me. And you take me in when you don't want to use me. What am I?'
'An anchor you throw it out of the ship to keep your ship still and you take it back when you want the ship to be able to move.'
'What 5 letter word becomes shorter when you add 2 letters to it.'
'short'
'Now Gerald your turn. The more of me here. The less you see me what am I?'
'Darkness.'
'You're riding the bus. On the 1st stop 5 women and 3 men come then on the 2nd stop 3 more women come and 1 woman and 1 man leave. On the 3rd stop 2 women leave and 3 men come. What is the color of the driver's hair?'
'Well, my hair's brown and I'm riding the bus so it's brown'
'Which word should you use to describe someone who doesn't have all his fingers on one hand?'
'Normal, because normal people have 5 on each hand.'
'Now Madson's turn. In some months there are 30 days and in some months there are 31 days what months have 28 days?'
'Every month'
'I'm tall when I'm young and I'm short when I'm Old. What am I?'

'A candle'
'You can catch me but never throw me. What am I?'
'Umm............. A cold?'
'Now it's Elijah's turn. What can travel around the globe but always stay in a corner?'
'A stamp'
'A duck was paid 11$, a bee was paid 33$ and a spider was paid 44$. How much was the dog paid?'
She thought and thought and thought. Time was ticking. And before she knew it, the answer sprang in his mind '22$, because the duck has 2 legs divided by two 1 and then a dog has 4 legs so divided by 2 is 2 so it's 22$'
'You're walking then you get kidnapped; you wake up in a basement with two guards guarding two doors. One door is safe and one door isn't. One guard always lies and one guard always tells the truth. They let you ask one question to both of them but it should be the same question. What must you ask to get to the safe door?'
'I don't know'
'If anyone else gets a question wrong all of you will be trapped in this room. And I will come out to do something. Now it's Evelyn's turn.'
'It had been raining and there were giant puddles on the pathway. There were three men on the pathway. They wanted to see who was the smartest. A random guy passing by offers to help. He has 3 black caps and 2 white caps he says that he will put on a cap on each of the men's heads when they close their eyes and they must try guessing the color without removing the hat or asking the others which color their hat was. So, they closed their eyes. The helper put the black caps on each of them and hid the white caps in his bag. One of them guessed the color of their hat how?'
'By looking at the puddle'

'I have 5 fingers but I'm not alive. What am I?'
'A hand'
'Wrong! Hahahahaha! Time to attack!'

The walls broke as some creatures entered the room; they were wearing black capes and Adeline couldn't see their faces through the hood. But she could see their teeth they were covered with blood and they were pointy. They were vampires! Adeline didn't waste her time; she ran as fast as she could. She then looked behind; her friends had been captured. The creatures were holding knives at their necks. Adeline shouted, 'NO!!! Don't kill them. I'll do anything, just leave them.'

One of the vampires said, 'Well, well you want to do anything to save your friends, Huh? Well, you see you have many powers and it's useless right now. We will make them useful. We'll kill the other 142 dwarves that we've captured. Just join our side. If you don't then all your friend's pretty heads will be gone.'

'Don't, Adeline just don't go on their side. He's a person who can control people he's controlling you to join them. Just don't.' Caliana said. But Adeline couldn't stand looking at all her friends die right in front of her and she also didn't want to join the other side. There had to be another way.

She couldn't beat 4 vampires! Finally, her history classes pay off. She had learned in her old human school that people believed that the vampire's skin would burn when touched with silver. She also always had a necklace her grandmother had given her a week before she kicked the bucket.

It was made from silver and it contained a pendrive with all the photos of her and her grandmother and that was the only thing that Adeline had about her. She took her necklace out. There were pointy stuff in the silver heart where the pendrive was also kept and all of them were made out of silver.

She took them and put them in her hands. Then she said in a sad tone, 'Can I at least see my friends before they go? I think I'll join your side. Now if I do join your side my powers will be useful and I won't be called 'the weird girl with 7 powers'. I'm sorry friends but this is such a good offer and it's also good for you guys you're safe, I'm safe, you're happy and I'm happy

'No don't join their side, Adeline! You know it's wrong.', Caliana said.

'Yes, and besides what will we explain to the adults? We won't be happy and we won't be safe too. With you, they'll be able to attack us easily. Do you realize why they haven't attacked Slopindon yet?

Because they have been waiting to recruit somebody like you. They were waiting and waiting and now that they have you, they'll attack Slopindon and they'll make you help them and we won't stand a chance. Please just don't join their side.' Madson said.

Adeline looked at them with an I know what I'm doing look and said, ' I don't care!'

She hoped her plan would work. She would first think of a wall and then make it appear between each vampire then pierce each of them with the sharp things. She took a deep breath in then said, 'I'll need to first conjure a wall between each of my friends. I want to talk to them a little privately. But only 1 vampire can be there.'

She first conjured brick walls between all the vampires high enough for them not to see through. Then she tried taking a sharp thing and then when she was looking at Caliana she pierced the sharp object in the vampire's heart. The vampire didn't move or scream.

She whispered to Caliana, 'I am acting as if I will join their side. I conjured a wall between the vampires so they wouldn't see me well do something to the vampire but I don't think I killed it so please be careful.'

Caliana smiled and said, 'I'll be fine I knew you were going to figure out something and you're acting almost convinced me until you gave me the I know what I am doing look. And I'm going to stay safe

Adeline did the same thing until she was done with all the vampires. Then all of them got up and were approaching the door but then Adeline said, 'Why go through the door it's locked anyways and it might take a lot of time and the vampires may wake up so I think it's safer to go by the walls. Who agrees with me?'. All 7 hands shot up in the air.

15

Then when they went out of the chaos, they entered another room but it was dark. The only light was coming from three different candles. Adeline tightened her grip on Caliana and Felicia.

'By the way, Adeline that was a really smart act. But why do you have spiky things in your pendant? It's just weird.', Madson said

'This is the only memory I have from my grandmother she died but a week before she passed away, she gave me this. It contains pictures and videos of me and her but since I entered Slopindon they don't use any gadgets so I can't see her photos and it pains me that I can't see my parents and now I miss my little sister Annie too.'

'Adeline, did you know that I saw you when you were little? People were trying to find you but nobody was able to. You might think Avery found you but no someone else found you. I had seen you but I didn't know you were an elf. Remember when you were 5 sitting in your garden reading a book? That day you saw a girl who was almost like your age that was me.', Caliana said.

'Who found me then?'

'My mother found you'

'How many people were spying on me'

'Me, my mother and Avery'

'That's a lot. Let's see how to get out of here now.'
They approached the three candles. It had a piece of paper on it. Adeline took the paper up and read it aloud, 'Find the 3 stars. Then when you're done put them in the box near the door. Then another paper will appear. Put that paper on the handle of the door and it will open.'
'Ok let's get to work we need to split into 3 groups. Caliana, Madson, and Adeline were in one. Bianca, Felicia, and Gerald were in one, and Evelyn and Elijah were in the other. They were putting siblings together.
Adeline took Caliana's hand and Caliana took Madson's hand. Then Adeline held the candle she made sure the light was distributed between the three of them.
They searched for a star, but there were no stars. 'Did anyone find a star?', Madson asked. The groups replied a sad no. T
hen something hit Adeline's mind. There might be stars in the box already the other survivor might have put them in the box.
She said, 'I think I know where it is, it might be in the box itself.'
They approached the door and surely the stars were in the box there was also a thick piece of paper. She put it on the door and the door opened.
'I think we should let Adeline do everything by herself who agrees she would do that easily?', Madson said.
'I mean she has 7 powers of course she would', Elijah said.
'Ya me too. But she only has 5 powers' said Bianca, Felicia, Evelyn, and Caliana at the same time, all of them looked at her and Adeline turned as red as the blood she had seen on the vampire's teeth.
'I do have 7 powers. I wanted to keep it a secret or else people would just call me 'the weird one with 7 powers' and

that's way worse than being called 'the weird one with 7 powers. Nobody in history had that many powers and the professor had also said that with great powers come great abilities. But how do you know that I have 7 abilities?' Adeline asked.

Everyone looked at Elijah and Adeline was glad that she wasn't in the middle of attraction anymore. Elijah said, 'Oh, I was passing by to the next class when I heard the professor saying you had 7 powers now.'

They entered the next room. It was a big ginormous room and it was full of keys. The door was at the end of the room. Adeline approached one key, her skin burned, and she felt like 1000 needles pierced her, and not only needles hot needles.

The others rushed to her. Felicia asked, 'What happened?'

'My hand burnt so bad when I touched the key. This is going to be hard. It doubles when you touch the wrong key. I can't get my hand burnt a million times that would be cretinous.'

'We'll take turns', Evelyn said. Evelyn approached a key. But it didn't burn her. It just multiplied. The same happened when Caliana approached another key. Now it was Bianca's turn the same happened to her.

Then Felicia went and the same thing happened to her. Nobody got burned. Why was she the only one?

Elijah went then Madson went then all of them had gone for a key and all of them had multiplied but still they hadn't gotten burned. It was now Adeline's turn.

She thought of which key to choose then she got an idea. She approached the key she had got burned with but Caliana and Evelyn took her arms and pulled her behind.

16

'WHAT DO YOU THINK YOU'RE DOING!', Caliana shouted.
She was so angry and it looked like her eyes were going to pop out.
'Come on I don't want to listen to another lecture you're pretty good at it you could go on for a whole day. You're worse than Mrs Brielle.', Madson said.
'Keep your mouth shut! And Adeline you still didn't answer my question. WHAT THE HELL WERE YOU DOING? You could have burnt your skin again and I'm telling you that is a severe burn. Is it still paining?'
'No, it isn't. And you were asking what I was doing well I figured that the keys that you guys have touched have not burned and only mine has burned.
And that might be because the key that burned is the correct key.
And besides it was not exactly like a burn it felt like hot needles piercing me.'
'Still. Wear these gloves before touching the key. They might help a little.'
Caliana took her gloves off and gave them to Adeline, Adeline took the gloves and wore them.
She then took the key and held it up it didn't multiply she went to the door and put the key in.
CLICK! The door opened. Adeline was proud of herself.

How many more doors would there be?
They entered the room. There was no time to think. Spikes were coming from the walls and they were like bullets they were shooting out of the wall every 3 seconds.
Adeline pondered what she should do. It was a long distance between the door and them they couldn't run.
This is where her powers come to use.
She took a deep breath in. Then she thought of a wall made of the strongest material.
Then she made the wall appear on the two sides of her. From the door to the other door.
Then they ran quickly but one spike fell from the ground. They dodged it. They were almost there.
Just 2 steps. Then they arrived there. But the door wouldn't budge when Adeline tried to open it.
There was a carpet underneath and she felt a lump in it she removed the carpet and found the key.
She got the key took it out and inserted it in the lock but it still didn't open. There was also a flower pot she dug the soil out but still no key.
She was lifting the pot to throw it because she was so angry but then she saw the key.
She took it out and put it in the lock. Finally, the door opened she ran to the next place. So far, the rooms were not easy but this one was so easy.
There was the door on the other side but to do that they had to go on the monkey bars but there were sharks below. That added more pressure. Caliana passed to the other side easily.
Caliana said, 'The door won't open there's also no place to hide the key to it we'll figure it out when you guys come you know Adeline figures everything out'
Bianca went next, she did it a little slow but as they say

slow and steady. Then Adeline went she decided to go from the top as it was way easier.

She couldn't even hang on a monkey bar for 5 seconds. Felicia went next followed by Gerald followed by Madson then Elijah, then Evelyn, but when Evelyn was halfway she fell. 'NO!', Elijah shouted.

Tears streamed down Elijah's cheeks. Madson tried to comfort him but Elijah would just push everybody who came close to him.

Adeline looked down. No sign of Evelyn.

17

Then she saw a face in the pool of sharks. Adeline read her mind turns out the sharks were shark holograms but they were not dangerous at all. She was not able to swim and she needed help.

Adeline was about to jump in when Caliana grabbed her hand. 'You're not going down there'. Adeline took some anxious moments and she became anxious when an icicle came in front of her she was lucky as this was a wide one. She then jumped down. She heard the others screaming at Adeline and she saw Caliana's angry, sad, and nervous face. She swam to Evelyn and took her hand. She dragged her to the side of the pool.

And got her out of the pool. Evelyn took a moment to gasp for air then said, 'Thanks so much! I was almost going to die. We need to get up

She replied, 'It's alright. And we don't need to get up they have to get down here I found something. But first I'll call them here,'

Adeline was never this proud. Suddenly she started levitating. Another power unlocked and this one was useful! She wished to go up and it went up and then she made it stop.

She explained what happened and Elijah was so glad that his sister was safe. All of them jumped down and went to

Evelyn. Elijah hugged her.

Then they all followed Adeline. They would have to swim but she decided not to risk Evelyn's life again.

She said, 'Okay do you guys trust me? Like trust me enough to make you guys fly without making you fall'

'Yep', they all replied.

They stood in a circle and started levitating. She went across the wide pool and then to the other side there was a tunnel lighted with torches. They entered the tunnel on the way there was a key she took it and then kept it in her pocket.

They walked for 5 more minutes. Then when they reached the end of the tunnel there was a door. She put the key in and the door opened. There was a room full of different potions.

She entered the room. When she reached the door there was a code no numbers or letters but colors. 3 colours. The walls started shrinking in. Adeline panicked, afraid she was going to make an icicle pop out of nowhere, she grabbed Caliana's hand and said, 'I'm claustrophobic I'll fill this place full of icicles if we don't get out of here.'

So, all of them took their hands and started searching the library but instead of books, there were potions. They searched and searched until they found a table with a scroll of paper on it.

Adeline opened the scroll and said, 'It's a potion recipe there are two potions whatever color the potion is the code to the door, to help us the potions are labeled. Well, I don't know this potion it says here that this potion is made from different potions for the first potion we'll need: Locka potion mixed with seethe potion. 4 people go to find that then come back here we'll mix it.

Do it as fast as possible because who would want to be

squished into the size of a paper I'm also Claustrophobic. Madson, Gerald, Elijah, and Evelyn in the team for the Seethe potion and Locka potion and the rest of us will find the Minitel potion and the Sith potion. Go!'

They ran to find the potions. Adeline used her levitating abilities to get higher to the top for a potion and the other they had no problem with. The other team's potions were both down so they didn't have to use their abilities.

They ran to the place where they had found two cauldrons and the piece of statue paper, they mixed it all. The first potion was blue and the second one was purple.

Adeline ran to the code and inserted blue then purple. The walls were closing in and she held tighter to Caliana's hand that she got hurt. Then, finally, the door opened.

The next room was like a beautiful garden and there were stone statues with perfect details that looked exactly like a person. 'Woah! These statues are too good!', Adeline said.'Yeah, as good as the statues Medusa makes!', Madson said laughing out loud.

'Yeah, that's true do you hear that?'-Caliana said, all of them fell silent and started listening. 'Chill! I was just kidding!', Caliana said.

'Well, me being me will still stay quiet. I mean look at this place, it might be Medusa's place. We need to be careful anyone have a mirror?', Adeline said.

'I do, I use it at school', Caliana said. Adeline took it and whispered, 'If Medusa is here, I'll be able to see her through this mirror without becoming a stone statue.'

'Gulp. Do you hear-r-r-r- th-th-th-that i-i-i think it-it's Me-medusa' Bianca said while shaking. 'Don't make a sound everyone. We need to get out of here all of us must go together. And absolutely no separation', Adeline whispered.

'HISSSS! New guests huh? Well, I get another stone statue. Yay! Where are you? SNIFF, hmm I think there is more than one person, probably 7 or 8. And one of you has a different smell of blood. Come on, get out of your hiding places cowards.', Medusa's voice said.

Adeline took out her mirror and told her friends to look down. They looked down. The place was full of stone statues. It made Adeline's skin crawl.

She looked at the mirror. She panicked.

18

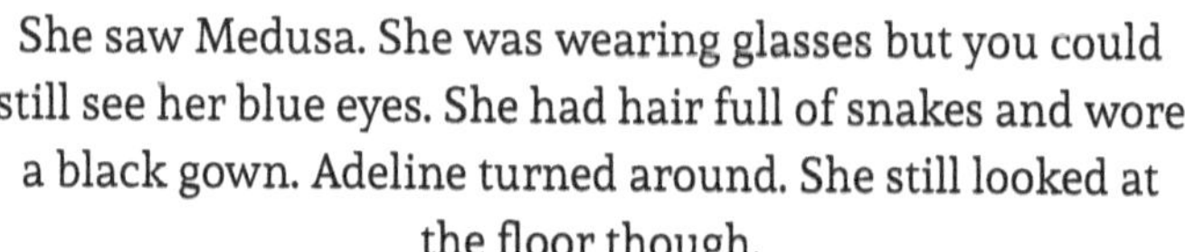

She saw Medusa. She was wearing glasses but you could still see her blue eyes. She had hair full of snakes and wore a black gown. Adeline turned around. She still looked at the floor though.

'Come on, look at me, little girl. You can join all of my different statues'

'No, I won't, how many statues have you made?', Adeline asked.

'You smell different.', Medusa said and she took off her glasses and said, 'Tempting to look at me isn't it? How long will you stare at the floor? Don't you think it's better to be turned into a stone statue than die?'

'It is tempting to look at you, but I'll pass. And I'd rather try to survive.', Adeline answered.

Medusa snorted, 'Yeah let's see if you last even for 5 seconds!'

Adeline took her sword from her back. And she charged for Medusa's neck. Medusa dodged her and ran away . Adeline told her friend to find the door. But they insisted on staying with her.

'Absolutely no separation, remember', Bianca said. Adeline sighed and told, 'Let's split into two groups. Who wants to come with me?'

Everyone's hands shot up. Adeline smacked her head. She

didn't want to let anyone down but still- she had to choose three people quickly- Medusa could come to attack anytime so she chose Felicia Madson and Caliana.
They followed the footprints in the soil and then they saw Medusa holding a pink crystal a little far away.
Medusa didn't notice them though and Adeline was relieved. She slowly took out her sword- so did the others. Caliana whispered, 'That pink crystal is not a good sign. You can teleport anywhere with that. Our green crystals on this gold bracelet can only teleport in Slopindon.'
Now Adeline panicked even more- her legs started to wobble but she kept them steady and then ran quietly to Medusa.
appeared behind her looking down. But she accidentally stepped on a slippery moss and slipped on it.
Medusa turned around. Adeline wobbled to her feet. She still looked down. Medusa took a knife from thin air and cut Adeline's skin on her right palm. Blood oozed out of her palm.
Medusa charged for Adeline and her friends. Now it was Adeline's turn to run away. She panicked but she wasn't nervous. She took her friend's hands. She ran and concentrated.
After a minute she started levitating. She ran and kept going up and up until she could see the whole garden. The sight was really painful to see- millions of stone statues were there- that also meant millions of miserable deaths.
She looked around and saw Evelyn, Felicia, Elijah, and Gerald near the door. They were beaming. They had opened the lock!
She went behind them and told Bianca, Caliana, and Madson to stay quiet. She went behind Evelyn, Felicia, Elijah, and Gerald. 'Boo!', she said. The four looked behind

taking out their swords.
Adeline hid her palms in her pocket, she wanted to hide it from her friends.
'Jeez! It's us. I see you have opened the lock. Come on we need to get out of here. We just escaped Medusa not kill her, she can teleport here anytime, she has a pink crystal.'
She pushed open the door. This room looked not dangerous at all but it looked impossible to escape it wasn't a room it was...

19

'This is an abandoned city, how the hell do we get out of here? And now I mean it absolutely no separations!', Adeline said.

She took Felicia's hand with her left palm but she couldn't hold Caliana's hand as it pained to touch anything with it. She put some cloth on it to cover it but Caliana had noticed it.

'What is that? You got hurt. Why didn't you tell me? How did you get hurt?', Caliana asked. 'I'm sorry I didn't tell you but it doesn't pain much. Medusa did this to me with her knife.', Adeline said. But it didn't look convincing that it didn't pain as Adeline started crying.

'Are you sure? You're crying. You have to rest look at the sky it's night, we have to sleep anyway.', Caliana said.

'And, that wound looks deep.', Madson added.

'Well, Adeline can just conjure some blankets, Beds, pillows, and a brick wall to protect us and a door in it with a lock and a key.', Bianca said.

'I'll try.', Adeline said.

She did it in a few minutes. 'Didn't I tell you; Adeline can do anything?', Madson beamed.

'We'll still need somebody awake. We'll take turns. I'll go first. I'll scream to wake you guys up.', Evelyn said.

Adeline went straight to sleep on the bed. She rested her

palm on the pillow.

Nightmares kept her awake. She thrashed around her bed. The dream was so bad.

She was in a garden; it was night the only light was coming from the moon and the flaming torches. She was being tortured. Cloaked figures were taking out her blood and keeping it in a veil.

Someone woke her up. She opened her eyes and saw Caliana near her. Caliana looked worried and she said, 'Adeline you were thrashing all around the bed, and look at your palm it's worse. Not only that, but your blood smells different. Medusa was right your blood is different.'

'I had a nightmare. What time is it?"

'It's 9:00.', Felicia said

'Oh my god! With a second we won't be able to bathe or eat!', Adeline almost shouted.

'Calm down, Felicia conjured some food. But it's impossible to conjure water.', Gerald said.

'I'm telling you guys that Adeline will be able to do it', Madson said.

'Yeah, I agree', Bianca said and beamed.

'I guess I'll give it a try.', Adeline said.

She thought of a bucket of water filled with water, but the bucket just appeared empty. Maybe it was impossible to conjure water. But she could control water. But that was only if some water was nearby. And the only water nearby was the bottled water in their bags. And they had to save that.

Then an idea popped into her mind. She hoped it would work.

20

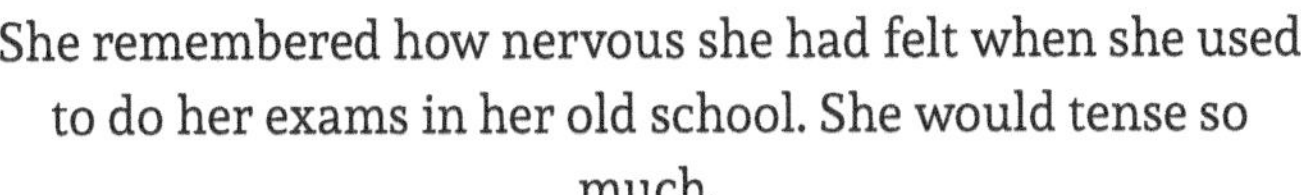

She remembered how nervous she had felt when she used to do her exams in her old school. She would tense so much.

Then she felt the feeling. she was feeling anxious. An icicle popped out of thin air. She conjured a bucket underneath the icicle.

She took her left-hand palm and put it in front. She remembered all the times she felt angry... when her sister had messed up with her homework and way more.

A spark came in her left hand she fed it with more angry moments and the fire grew in her palm. The fire was as big as her head. She shot it at the icicle.

The icicle slowly started melting and the water was collected in the bucket.

She conjured more buckets as the icicle was big enough to fill 10 giant buckets.

They bathed and then went back to bed to eat the food that Felicia had conjured.

Then Adeline snapped her fingers and the things disappeared. They took each other's hands just like they had in the beginning.

Then they continued to walk. There were buildings covered with moss, dead trees, shrivelling plants, barks with moss growing on them, and rocks with moss.

This was so green. Adeline wondered how it looked long ago. 'This looks like a place where humans live. The air is so polluted. There are so less trees in here. I wonder how they live.

They type these buttons and everything. When I was smaller, I saw these things they called factories. It was so brutal to the plants.', Caliana said.

Adeline looked around the place looked like it was in the human world itself. Adeline told her friends that maybe they should check the buildings. So, they went to one.

The door had no lock, so the door opened. She looked inside to see if it was safe. There was no one to be seen. They climbed the stairs cautiously. Avoiding places with moss.

Then they kept climbing the stairs until they found a door. She opened it. It was a house! This looked recently made and used. There were fresh muddy footprints and leftover food on the table.

She continued in the room and found a bedroom. It looked new. The bed looked like it was never used. Adeline opened the wardrobe. New clothes! But it was weird there were exactly 6 pairs of clothes and 2 dresses. It was like whoever lived here knew that they would come here.

They took turns to change.

Adeline felt fresh. She was wearing loose blue jeans and a black crop top. Adeline was the first to change. She was so happy to wear human clothes again.

Felicia went next. She came outside in a red dress and said, 'I hate human clothes the clothes are a little rough.'

That was true dwarves' clothes were way softer. Bianca wore a blue jean with a black top. Evelyn wore a red dress a little similar to Felicia. Caliana got the wrong dress. She came out of the room disgusted. She was wearing black torn jeans and a light blue crop top. She said, 'Why are my jeans torn?'

Adeline laughed and said, 'That's what humans call fashion'

'That's stupid', Caliana said.

Madson wore a black jean and a blue shirt. Elijah wore the same jeans and a green t-shirt and Gerald wore dark blue jeans with a white shirt.

They searched the room but found nothing else. They went to the next room it was a bedroom again. On the bed was a note.

'Find the 3 stars. Insert them in the thing near the door.', Adeline read aloud. 'Well, we better get to work.' Let's split into 3 groups. Sibling groups. Me, Adeline and Madson. Felicia, Gerald, and Bianca. Evelyn and Elijah. When you're done your star meet up at the door. But if you can't find anything don't search too long and come back to the door maybe we already found them. I'll show you where it is.', Caliana said.

She went out of the house. There was another door next to it; the exit door.

They split into their teams and started searching for the stars.

21

Adeline wondered how Caliana knew where the door was but she decided not to ask. She wondered around the place. Then she saw a tree bark which was empty inside she went to search in it but there was no star there. But could she have meant the stars in the sky?

'Is there any way we can get a star from the sky?', Adeline asked.

'Yes, we use this telescope kind of thing to capture them.', Madson said.

'We had to bring one to class yesterday so I have one in my bag', Caliana said.

She took it out of her bag and landed it on Adeline. Adeline took the telescope and asked, 'How do we use it?'

'Well first you take it align it to the star you want then tighten the grip and the star will go in the telescope. You need to then transfer it into a veil which is the hard part, your hand might burn in the process.', Caliana said.

'And we're not letting you do that part', Madson added.

Adeline captured the star and handed it to the twins. They took out a veil out of their bag and then they transferred it into the veil. The process didn't look like it would burn someone at all.

She captured two more stars and then Caliana took 2 more veils out of her bag and then Madson transferred them into the veil.

'You'll have to conjure some thick gloves we can't hold these hot veils without them it would burn our skin so badly.', Caliana said.

Adeline conjured some thick gloves and handed them to them. They wore them and each of them wore one pair. They took a veil each and headed to the door.

Adeline opened the veils and the stars leaked out of it like water and the door clicked open. The others were there. They looked depressed. Bianca said, 'We haven't found anything have you?'

'Yep! We found all of them come on we opened the door let's go!', Adeline said. She pushed open the door. It was a big field. The field was as big as the garden in High Peaks. It had 4 flags. They were standing near the blue flag.

Adeline knew what was happening; they would be playing protectors and taggers. 8 people in each group and they would be in blue. There were 8 dwarves near each flag.

A voice shouted, 'Welcome! We're going to be playing the game with protectors and taggers.8 dwarves in each group. Whoever's team captures a flag and all their taggers win. The team that hasn't captured a flag and its taggers and protectors will lose. All powers are allowed. You have 10 minutes to discuss your plan. If you lose you die.'

Adeline felt like the voice sounded a little similar but she ignored that. They started discussing the plan.2 people attacked the taggers, 3 people captured a flag and 3 people protected the flag.

Adeline, Bianca, and Felicia would be capturing Red's flag as it was the closest. Evelyn and Elijah would be attacking the flag. Caliana, Madson, and Gerald would be protecting the flag.

Adeline noticed 2 faces between the people in green; Alden

and Alina! They were captured too. If one person's team won 8 innocent people would die! Adeline couldn't let that happen and Alden and Alina might be one of them.

The game was not fair. How many creatures would come to kill the 24 dwarves? If they were more than 10, they wouldn't be able to kill them. Adeline and her friends started discussing what to do if people came to kill.

First of all, they would scream, 'Everybody! Attack! Defend yourselves!' Then maybe their numbers would even out. Whenever they screamed now, they would circle a creature and then attack.

The plan wasn't good though. A whistle blew, and time was up. Adeline covered the flag with 200 cm long fire so there was extra protection. Then Adeline looked at the red flag 3 people were protecting the flag.

Adeline, Bianca, and Felicia would be capturing Red's flag as it was the closest. Evelyn and Elijah would be attacking the flag. Caliana, Madson, and Gerald would be protecting the flag.

Adeline noticed 2 faces between the people in green; Alden and Alina! They were captured too. If one person's team won 8 innocent people would die! Adeline couldn't let that happen and Alden and Alina might be one of them.

The game was not fair. How many creatures would come to kill the 24 dwarves? If they were more than 10, they wouldn't be able to kill them. Adeline and her friends started discussing what to do if people came to kill.

First of all, they would scream, 'Everybody! Attack! Defend yourselves!' Then maybe their numbers would even out. Whenever they screamed now, they would circle a creature and then attack.

The plan wasn't good though. A whistle blew, and time was

up. Adeline covered the flag with 200 cm long fire so there was extra protection. Then Adeline looked at the red flag 3 people were protecting the flag.

73

22

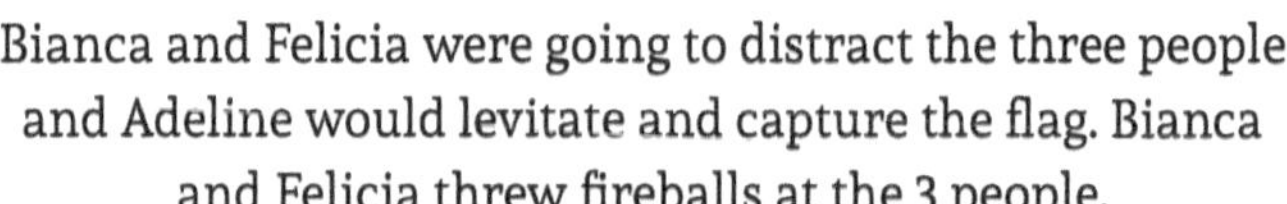

Bianca and Felicia were going to distract the three people and Adeline would levitate and capture the flag. Bianca and Felicia threw fireballs at the 3 people.
Adeline started levitating she went towards the flag and then captured it. Evelyn and Elijah were not having good luck. They went to help them. Adeline screamed Now! They cornered three of the 5 taggers. Then each of them pounced on the taggers. Two more to go.
They ran to the last two of the taggers. When they reached them, they cornered them. They pounced and then they won!
Now they had to wait to attack once again. After 15 minutes the voice said, 'The loser is Green. Soon, dwarves will enter to kill them. Red, Blue, and Yellow you can exit.'
Green had lost! Alden and Alina were on that team. She looked at Caliana and Madson and said, 'Green lost! Alden and Alina are in there if we lose this fight and let those dwarves kill them 8 innocent people will die and 2 of them are our parents! We can't let that happen.'
'To the exit now!', the voice shouted.
'No! We need to save them', Adeline shouted.
'Oh, it's you. The one they have been talking about. You know little girl, if you don't go, I'll make you go there. Now be a good girl, And Get Out! And you know- you're the one

who's causing all of this. They want others and you mainly. You'll see what I mean, now. Get. Out. Of. Here.'
Adeline had a plan but she had to act for now, but before getting out of there she had to ask 3 questions to whoever the person speaking was.
She asked, 'But I have three questions before I get out of here, how many dwarves will come to kill?'
'28 and very skilled ones.'
'Ok. Who are you? It's almost like I know you, you sound similar.'
'No, you don't know me! And you don't have to know.', the voice said. Adeline wondered why he had told that answer so tensely. She knew this person.
'Alright, maybe I don't know you. So, the last question before I get out of this exit is- Who are my parents?'
'I won't tell you.'
'So, you know but you won't tell me?'
'You don't have to know about them but I must say you look familiar to them. Those blue eyes and that brownish hair'
'You knew them?'
'Yes, I did'
'So, tell me who they are! Two names that's all I'm asking for. There's no harm if you tell me two names, right?'
'You don't have to know how many more times I have to tell you that?'
'OF COURSE, I NEED TO KNOW! THEY'RE MY PARENTS! JUST TELL ME!'
'Get out of the exit, the dwarves are coming soon, they'll kill anybody who they see.'
'I won't get out until you answer my question.'
'GET OUT!'
'FINE! I'll figure out who they are myself. Idiot.'

'I'm not an idiot once you see how smart I am and who I am you'll be surprised and you won't hurt me I just know that.'

23

Adeline frowned and her eyebrows met. She wondered who the person talking was, she did sound familiar but now she had no time to think. The dwarves were going to arrive soon.

The door burst open and 28 bulky dwarves arrived out of it. "Everybody! Attack! Defend yourselves!', Adeline screamed. She took out her sword; so did the others.

She put her shield up and charged for one of the dwarves. She looked at it a little closer these were dwarf holograms. But not like the ones she used to practice with at High Peaks. Their button to turn them off was not there.

She remembered when she was doing fighting lessons the professor had told her that there were two types of dwarf holograms. One type had a button on its waist and the other in its literal head.

The dwarf holograms only worked for 1 person but you could change the person who they listen to when you go to the button in the head press it 10 times and tell the name of the person the dwarf hologram should listen to.

She took out her sword and tried to stab it in the dwarf's heart, but he blocked it with a wall of fire. Adeline removed it with some water.

She then levitated and attacked for its head, but the dwarf blocked it with another wall of fire.

She was getting impatient now. She removed the fire with more water. Before the dwarf could do anything, she collected more air and threw it at the dwarf. The dwarf fell over.

She went to attack the dwarf but he got up and conjured another wall of fire. She then had an idea to make him stop using his powers. Her teacher had made her use them when she was fighting once to see if she was good at fighting without powers.

Adeline stepped away from the dwarf and then closed her eyes. She pictures the Hola hoop-looking thing that was blue with pink crystals on it. She then threw it around the dwarf.

The dwarf was now not able to use his powers. Adeline took her sword and charged for the dwarf. She stabbed it in the head. Then the button showed up. She smacked it ten times and said, 'Adeline'

The dwarf started healing itself and now it was looking as healthy as it was before. She commanded, 'Go attack the other dwarf holograms, Peter'

She had asked his name so she could give commands from far away. She looked around, everyone was fighting.

She went to a dwarf hologram; a little girl was fighting with it and she had no chance of winning so she went to help. She ran to them as fast as she could so she could save the girl before the dwarf killed her.

She ran as fast as she could but then her heart froze; she saw her body lying down blood dripping out of her chest. Tears streamed down Adeline's cheek but there would be more people ending up like this if she didn't kill that hologram.

She wanted revenge. She reached the dwarf. She ran behind the hologram as quietly as possible by levitating.

Then she lowered herself to ground level.

She stabbed the sword in the head. The button pressed up 'she did the same thing she had done with Peter; she smacked the button 10 times and said; 'Adeline' The head healed up instantly.

Adeline couldn't resist saying, 'Woah' She asked, 'What's your name?"

'Amen'

'Ok, Amen go attack the other holograms except Peter.' Amen ran off and Adeline looked at the little girl's body and then around. Blood. Blood. Blood, she had never seen so much blood. Bodies were lying down too. But luckily none of them were Alina and Alden.

She looked around to see Bianca and Felicia fighting three dwarves so she went to help them. She took out her sword then she ran to the dwarf hologram. She kept her shield up. The dwarf didn't have any shield so that made it easier for Adeline to kill it. Kinda. She had learned a fighting technique in fighting lessons. She was not too good at it but she decided to do it anyway.

She took her legs up and hit the dwarf in its guts then she took her shield and pushed it in its stomach. She then took her shield and banged it on its head. The dwarf was not fine at all. But it still had life in it.

Good enough life to fight. The dwarf turned out to have conjuring skills so it conjured a shield. Adeline conjured a thick and long rope. She took both of its ends and threw it over the dwarf.

Then she tugged on it; this was going to be a little hard; the hologram was heavy. The dwarf conjured a knife and then cut the rope. Adeline didn't know how to kill this dwarf. Then the dwarf took his shield out of its arms. Adeline took her opportunity and aimed for its head. The head split and

the button got out she smacked it 10 times and promptly
said, 'Adeline'
'what's your name?'
'Talena'
'Go attack the bad holograms.'

24

Adeline then saw Bianca and Felicia approaching her. Bianca said, 'There were 32 people before…. Now there are only 29 left. And one of them is…. Evelyn.'

'What?!' said a voice behind Adeline.

Elijah was crying there. He said, 'Is she dead? Sniff. I-I-mean la-la st time she was not-not dead.' He struggled to say each word.

'I'm sorry Elijah but she's dead. But she died fighting. I saw her fighting with a dwarf and then she killed it. Then she saw 10 dwarves attacking 8 dwarves. She went to save them. Then one of the 10 dwarves said if she sacrificed her life then they would leave the 8 people. So, she did.', Felicia said.

Adeline couldn't bear it. She needed revenge. She had a plan. But if it would work, she didn't know. But she decided to follow her instincts. She thought of a bomb that would blast the whole room. She took a deep breath and then shouted, 'Everybody to the exit right now. We must escape!' Everyone rushed to the exit. But Adeline stayed for a while.

'Adeline! Come!', Felicia shouted.

Adeline said, 'One second.'

She threw the ball in the middle of the room and then rushed to the exit. Then she conjured an indestructible wall in the gap from the room. Then a blasting sound came.

Adeline covered her ears. Then she looked around and saw Alina and Alden. She went to hug them. She flung her arms around them. Madson and Caliana joined.

'I was so worried about you guys. More than I was about myself.', Alina said.

'We made it out fine but many people out of the 32 didn't make it. There were 10 deaths.', Madson said.

'I feel so sorry for them.', Alden said.

'Me too.', Caliana said.

'Me three', Alina said.

Adeline wrapped her two arms around herself and then said, 'Evelyn was one of the 10 ones to be gone.'

There was a sad silence then someone broke it in the 22 people, 'Ok we need to get out of here'

That was Avery. 'Everyone split into 3 groups. In two of them 7 people and in one 8.', Aveline's voice shouted.

They sorted in 3 groups Adeline was with Alina, Alden, Madson, Caliana, Bianca, Felicia, and Elijah. She was in the middle of the line. Behind her was Bianca and in front Felicia.

There were three lines. They went to the next door and entered it. It was night now. The moon was shining. And they were in a gloomy garden. Adeline felt like she had been here once. Her head pained.

Bianca asked, 'Adeline are you okay? You're shaking.'

Adeline nodded. She studied herself.

A hooded person walked in front and everyone took out their swords ready to charge. The hooded person said, 'Don't worry, I won't harm you unless Adeline comes with us. We'll give her back after some time. But first, you need to give me Adeline. If you don't, I'll kill all of you guys.'

Adeline was afraid to go. She stayed there and didn't budge.

Then, she uncontrollably walked forward a few steps. The hooded person was controlling her.

Felicia and Bianca pulled Adeline backward. Adeline was forced to get out of their grasp and head to the hooded person. The hooded person said, 'Everyone go back to the door and go to the place you came from.'

They didn't budge. But then the hooded person controlled them to the exit. He took Adeline's hand. She had no chance she could escape his hand. It was like iron.

The hooded person took her further into the garden. The place looked like a graveyard. It had graves. There was also a cauldron and a wall which looked like a place they used to hang people by their head.

There were people in a circle behind the cauldron. Adeline tried to look at their faces but all of them had a hood over them.

25

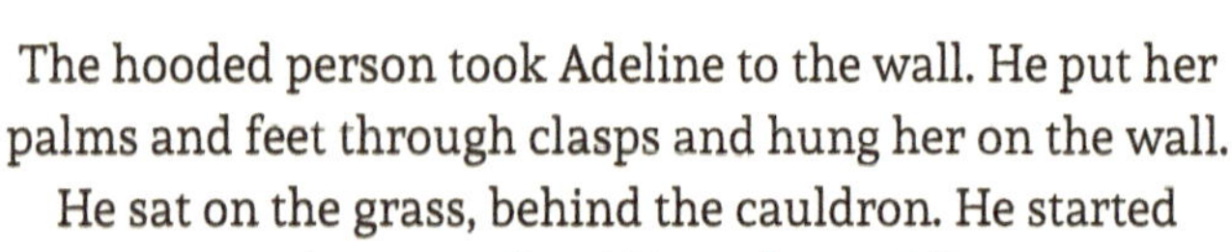

The hooded person took Adeline to the wall. He put her palms and feet through clasps and hung her on the wall. He sat on the grass, behind the cauldron. He started pouring some liquid into the cauldron.
Some green sludgy thing, purple liquid, some powder, and some round things which dissolved in the potion. He stirred the potion with a long wooden stick.
He looked at Adeline and took out a knife. Adeline panicked. He said, 'Well, well, well you can't escape now. You might know that you have special blood. You're the only one with this type of blood. I'll just need 3 drops of blood and you're free to go.'
Adeline closed her eyes and held her breath as the hooded person approached her. Adeline thought that he would cut her skin but instead, he tortured her. He forced Adeline to drink a potion. Adeline chugged the whole potion bottle. Minutes passed and nothing happened. Then, suddenly, it felt like her body was being crushed. Then screaming voices shouted so loud in her ears. Her head started to pain. Adeline screamed she couldn't explain the pain, but it was so bad.
She took a deep breath in and tried to shove away all the feelings. But it wouldn't go away. 'STOP IT!', she screamed. No replies came back.

After a few minutes of suffering, the feeling stopped.
Adeline let out a sigh of relief.
She opened her eyes. The hooded person approached
Adeline and cut a deep slash in Adeline's palm. She
screamed and shouted, 'You only need 3 drops of my blood.
Why such a deep cut?'
Again, no replies. She hated this behavior. But now she was
getting used to it. Nobody was telling her who her
biological parents were.
He put the drops in the cauldron and mixed it with the
long wooden spoon. The potion started to fume.
It became purple. He stored it in a vile. He removed the
chains and set Adeline free. She looked at the deep slash in
her palm.
She ran to the place where the others were. She hid her
pam because she didn't want the others to worry about it,
especially Calian, Alden, and Alina.
She pushed open the door to see 7 anxious people waiting
for her; Alden, Alina, Caliana, Madson, Elijah, Felicia and
Bianca. 'Are you ok?', they all asked her.
Adeline answered, 'Yes. Fine'
'It looks like you're lying, Adeline. We also heard you
scream. Show me your hands, you've been hiding it as soon
as you came to the door.', Alina said.
Adeline hesitated, but she showed her palm.
Alden said, 'That's such a deep cut. We'll have to put some
cloth on it.' He took a handkerchief from his pocket
wrapped it around Adeline's palm and asked, 'Does it still
pain a lot?'
'No', Adeline said.
'What else happened in there? I know they wouldn't take
that much time to cut your skin', Alina
'Nothing', Adeline said in a kind of convincing voice.

Everyone's eyebrows shot up. "You guys won't let me alone until I tell you, will you?" They nodded.

Adeline sighed and said, 'They tortured me. They forced me to chug a potion. Nothing happened in the beginning. But after some time, it felt like my body was being crushed. Then screaming voices shouted so loud in my ears. My head started to pain. I can't explain the pain, but I can tell you one really clear thing. It was so bad.'

Alden and Alina looked worried and looked at each other.

'What happened?', Adeline asked.

Alden said, 'That potion is a potion created to torture people. Now that you drank it, you might get that feeling and all your energy will go anytime for the next 2 days.'

Adeline gaped.

'Come on we need to continue!', Avery said.

Adeline followed Bianca. Then, all the energy drained from her body. She fell to the ground. Ringing and screaming voices came in Adeline's ears. All the air in her body was crushed and it felt like she was being stabbed with a million spikes. She felt like she was being crushed. Adeline screamed. All the 7 people came back to check on her. Adeline wrapped her hands around her legs and shut her eyes. She couldn't explain the pain again but, it was worse than last time.

After a few minutes, it stopped to pain. Adeline let out a sigh of relief. Tears rolled down her cheeks. This was going to happen for 2 days! She looked up it was night.

They went to sleep.

26

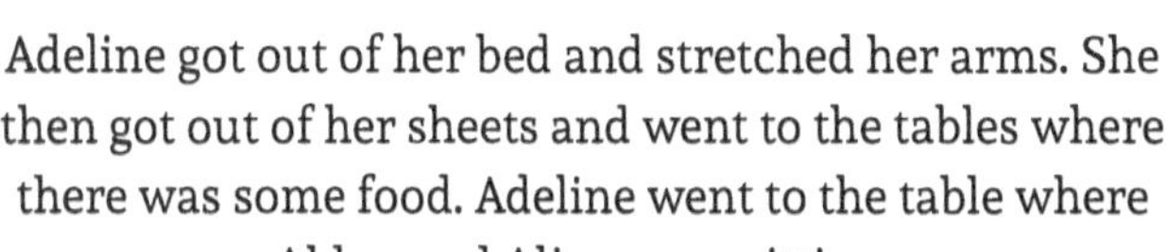

Adeline got out of her bed and stretched her arms. She then got out of her sheets and went to the tables where there was some food. Adeline went to the table where Alden and Alina were sitting.

Not many people had woken up, only 10 people. Adeline checked her watch it was 4:59. She was still sleepy though. She wanted to sleep more but she was afraid she would have way more nightmares.

"Good morning, youngster! How's it going?", Alina asked.

Adeline sighed and replied, 'Not good, we're stuck in a maze, we got out from a fight where so many people were killed, and one who was my friend. Evelyn was lucky once when she was drowning, she was close to dying. But this time we did lose her. Elijah is so sad.'

'I know. It's hard. But we can't keep on crying about people's death. We need to move on. We need to escape the maze. It is really hard, about 9000 years ago only one man survived, so it's pretty hard. Are you sure you don't want to get some more minutes of sleep? You look quite tired and you have black lines under your eyes. Yesterday was also really tough for you", Alden said.

Adeline shook her head and said, 'I am NOT going back to sleep. I had too many nightmares last night. I hope whatever coming ahead in this maze is not too bad.'

"BOO!". Adeline jumped. She took her sword out and turned around ready to stab the sword in the person. Then she got relieved, it was just Madson and Elijah. They loved to joke around.

'Jeez, Adeline, be careful with that sword of yours you were just about to kill me! And by the way, I need a special award. Look at the time I woke up early! 'Madson said settling on a chair.

Elijah took a chair and sat there. 'You do not deserve an award. I think Adeline deserves one and not only one or two!', Bianca, Felicia, and Caliana said together from behind. It was so perfect it was almost like they had rehearsed it.

Adeline jumped once more and was taking out her sword when Madson took her hand and said, 'Oh little sister, you're not trying to stab your friends and sibling again are you? It's just Bianca, Felicia and Caliana. I know you're good with swords and you've been only practicing for 1 week. But it doesn't mean you need to use it all the time!'

The three settled next to Adeline. Felicia said, 'Come on, Madson is just jealous that Adeline is better at fighting than him and she had only been practicing for some weeks and he has been practicing for 2 years. Who else agrees?'

Everyone's hand raised except Madson, instead he said, 'I'm not jealous. I was just making sure you guys wouldn't be cut into slices with Adeline's amazing skills'

'So even you are saying that Adeline's better than you. See!', Bianca said.

'Plus, everyone saw how good Adeline fought in the battle. She fought 3 dwarf holograms and I bet all of us fought 2 or only one!', Caliana added.

'Plus, everyone agrees that there's something special in Adeline. 'Alden and Alina added

'And last of all, Adeline's blood is special. Medusa told it when we saw her. And those stupid cloaked figures needed your blood only, that means you are special.', Elijah added up at last.

Madson said, 'I'm not jealous. I'm just proud that my little sister learned her sword skills from me.'

'First of all, stop calling me little sister and call me by my name, that's why we have names. And, second of all, you never taught me anything.', Adeline said.

'Okay, okay. All of you stop talking, eat your food we're going in 15 minutes. We need to keep ourselves armed that will take about 8 minutes, so eat a little quickly, but, don't choke over your food.', Alina said.

Adeline gobbled up her food so fast, then she went to get ready. After a moment, they all gathered up and went to the next door.

27

The strong wind swept upon the faces. Adeline struggled to keep her eyes open for at least a few seconds. Adeline fainted and then woke up to be able to open her eyes properly. She looked around, she was in a room, there was a window and through it she saw that each of the other 28 people was in the same situation as her, they were trapped.

But Adeline just knew there was a key somewhere in the room. She then realised it was not a room it was a whole house. There was a key on the floor, Adeline knew it wouldn't be that easy.

She took the key and opened the door and entered the next room. Adeline gasped, there was a huge chessboard in Infront of her. A voice said, 'I will be playing a game of chess with you, you're white, just shout out what you want to play and it will play for you. You need to choose a piece to be on, if that piece gets captured, then you die. I'll give you 2 minutes to think, if you win then you'll get the key to the next room.'

Adeline was not too good in chess so she was scared. Then, an idea popped in her clever mind, if she took the king there was no chance, she could die as the king can't get captured. So, she took that piece and the game began. Adeline wasn't too good at chess she had no idea how to play it and she didn't even know how the pieces moved. Her best friend in New York where she used to live was very good in chess and always kept talking about it to Adeline so she hoped she could win this game.

Adeline's heart beat and her hand shook when she went to take the place on the king.

Adeline lost but the opponent couldn't attack her king so he got the key. She opened the next door.

She saw a dazzling light a little far away. She started walking towards it. The closer she got the less bright the light became. When she got close, she understood what it was. It was a diamond necklace. Because of her greediness, she went to take it. But when she touched it, something really strange happened. Adeline felt so light and she was in the sky.

After a few minutes, she landed with a loud thud. She looked around, she was in a house, the house was full of webs, and spiders and barely had any furniture. The only objects inside were some skulls, bones, and a really old chair with a lot of moss on it. Adeline was terrified. What was this place and was there anyone else except me? She dared not to speak. One of her questions got answered when a lady entered the room.

She had a long nose, she was tall, she wore a black cloak and her hair was black and curly. she froze because she was scared out of my wits. The lady said, 'Oh we have a new visitor! I've been getting lonely lately, it's nice to have young visitors like you.' Adeline kept my mouth shut. The lady said, 'OK let me introduce myself, I'm Pathfinder. Nothing to be afraid of me is there?'

Adeline managed to whisper some words, 'B-b-b-but why do you have skulls and blood in your house?' 'Who told you this is my house? I got here just like you, I saw something shining, I went towards it and when I touched it teleported me here and it was my biggest regret in my whole life. This is an evil person's house. she tortures everyone she captures at night. I've been here for 3 weeks and it's miserable, the witch doesn't even give me food. I have a plan to escape but it's risky. I have been waiting for someone else to come so I could carry out my plan. Do you want to join my plan? I think I already know your answer. And also introduce yourself please.'

Adeline was glad that she wasn't evil or anything. She was also happy she had a plan to escape. Adeline immediately said, 'Of course, I would love to! And I'm sorry for you. My name is Adeline. I am in 7th grade and I'm 11 years old.' 'The witch tortures us one by one on the chair. I will be the first one, when I'm getting hard jobs, you will have to stay in the other room. The witch will take a sword and slash me everywhere it's really painful, that's why I have these marks So that's how it's supposed to be. But, that's not my plan.'

She gave Adeline a slingshot and Pathfinder told her the plan, it was simple, but Adeline was scared for one part. Finally, night came. Adeline went out of the room with my slingshot and paper in her pocket. When it was time, she shot the witch. She turned around and looked at Adeline. She was so red. Without losing any time, Adeline ran as fast as I could. She looked behind her and the witch was catching up quickly.

She looked at Pathfinder with worried eyes and shouted, 'NOW!' Pathfinder took the rope wrapped it around the witch, and tied her to the chair. She tied her hands and legs, then she took out the key from the witch's pocket. They both went to the exit door and unlocked it.

28

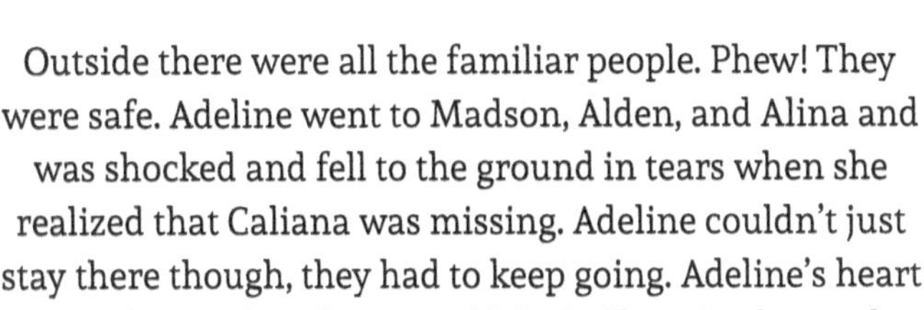

Outside there were all the familiar people. Phew! They were safe. Adeline went to Madson, Alden, and Alina and was shocked and fell to the ground in tears when she realized that Caliana was missing. Adeline couldn't just stay there though, they had to keep going. Adeline's heart was broken and nothing would fix it. She wiped away her tears and got up.

Avery came to Adeline and said, 'Umm... Adeline can I talk with you, nothing serious don't panic

'Sure', Edaine replied waving her hand to the others.

'We'll wait', Alden said with a smile that glued a little part of her heart together.

'Adeline, well first thing everybody's insisting that you to lead us, I know the responsibilities are really heavy but I agree with them, you're really strong, and in all of us you're the best in fighting and you'll make the best decisions. Second of all, we weren't friends before, but, what about now?'

'Yes', Adeline managed a smile.

'You know, even though we're in severe danger right now, we have a chance to figure out who these people are, 9000 years ago the people weren't able to figure out who they were, maybe they did but they didn't survive to come back only one person came back from there and he soon died only saying a few words which left us with a clue what had happened but we only knew a little information. Our history and Slopindon aren't calm anymore. I believe that Slopindon is no longer safe for us. This voice speaking every time doesn't it sound similar to you?'

'Yes, it does though I can't make out who it is. As soon as I came to this maze my mind hadn't been functioning too well and it was hard to even get a good night's sleep. Sometimes I'm on the bed looking up at the roof and think what would happen if I stayed in New York City, I miss my family, even though my little sister always messed with me she was always there with me she loved me, and cared for me. And I can't believe I'm saying this but I also miss school. Sometimes I just stare in disbelief and try to convince myself this isn't true. But I know it is. And I can't believe all these 11 years I have been trapped in a world with no magic and right in front of me was a world full of magic and all these years I wasn't living with my biological parents and I still have no idea who they are.'

'It's hard to believe how I could live without my parents. We'll figure out who is that person speaking every time and 100% we'll figure out who your parents are. And I'm sorry for your loss, it's going to be like this though so we need to adjust.'

Adeline turned her back and was about to leave when Avery said, 'And Adeline, remember, if you need me I'm always there.'

Adeline thanked her and waved.

Adeline thought, 'I should stay firm I'll have way more, losses. And more mysteries.' Adeline and the others went to the next door and pushed it open.

It was the ocean. On the sandy beach was a huge ship Adeline was confused of why the ship was there. She was now the leader of the whole 29 so she went in front and studied the ship, no one was in there.

So, she marched onto the ship. Adeline's suspicions grew. The ship was loaded with weapons. Then it hit Adeline's mind. It was a naval battle. She thought about what could have happened to Caliana and she thought of something but just thinking of it hurt her mind.

Adeline was not ready for this; she couldn't fight she was not as good as the others. She had only practiced fighting for 3 weeks and that wasn't enough, but she fought through all the ifs and buts and made up her mind, she only had one thing in her head: You have and can do this! Well, at least that stayed for 1 minute because something came to her mind, she had no idea how to put the ship to the sea, she had no idea how to use these weapons and how would she steer the ship? The questions stormed in her mind and wouldn't get away.

She struggled and shoved them away.

29

'Wow Madson you're serviceable!', Bianca beamed with a cheeky grin.

'Yeah, I think only Mrs Midson I useful, right? Well, look at me I just put the ship to sea!', Madson said returning Bianca's grin.

Bianca's eyebrows scrunched and almost touched each other, she was bewildered, 'Who the hell is Midson?'

'Well, you're not the sharpest tool in the shed, are you? Midson is Adeline's last name.'

'Oh, silly me! I didn't even ask Adeline's last name.', Bianca hit her head with her hand.

Someone cleared their throat. Bianca looked behind to see a ruffled hair Adeline.

'What happened to you?', Madson asked pointer his finger at Adeline.

'Well, we got the ship on sea but I can't find someone who can drive this ship, I can't even find the place to drive the ship whenever I ask someone they just look confused.', Adeline said.

'Nincompoop, In Slopindon we use magic to do that no wonder everyone was so confused.', Madson said.

'What did you just call me?', said Adeline losing her temper.

'I was just kidding.', Madson replied.

A spark of fire came in Adeline's hand, but, before it could grow too big and burn down the whole ship, Elijah and Felicia came to the rescue. They both coincidentally threw water at the same time to put out the fire and Adeline came back to normal. One thing she liked is that she had made some friends throughout the journey and she was no longer the shy person she used to be.

'Adeline! Be careful! You were about to burn down this ship!', Bianca busted out.

'Sorry', Adeline whimpered.

'It's alright, Adeline, we learn from our mistakes.', Madson said.

'Yes, but just don't do it next time', Felicia added.

'I'm going to put the spell on the ship.', Elijah said and rushed off.

After a few minutes, the ship started moving. Adeline announced, 'Everybody gathers up in the front of the ship, I'm coming.' And with that, she rushed to the front. She had just learned how to use the weapons now she felt confident.

She said, 'Everyone here knows how to use weapons right?' Everybody nodded. Adeline was glad, 'Good, Alden, Alina, Avery, Madson, Felicia, Juliette, and Bianca you control the cannons and I'll control one too. Little girl with the blue top and white jeans and the other 4 adults around her your job is to help everyone to reload their guns. Elijah and Pathfinder you go to the top of the ship and if you see any sign of danger through the binoculars you alert us by using the bell. Miss Brielle, Jennie, Mr Jones, and Catherine, you can control the bombs. The rest you shoot the enemy with the guns.'

Adeline went to the cannon next to Avery. There were 8 cannons in all. They finally left the shallow tides and could barely see the land anymore. The adventure was only starting now though.

The sun went down and the moon replaced it and Adeline noticed something strange about it there seemed to be a huge black dot on it. Well turns out it wasn't a huge dot it was a huge flock of birds coming to attack them.

Everyone scattered and shouted as the pigeons attacked them with their beaks. Adeline shouted over the noise, 'Nobody attack them with your weapons. We'll just waste it. Who knows how to make the sound of a hawk? When I say go whoever knows how to make the sound make it, pigeons are afraid of hawks, so this might work. One, Two, Three and GO!'

Adeline covered her ears but that wasn't enough to block the huge noise that the people were making. Fortunately, the pigeons left us and we were in peace, for now.

The sea became rough and the weather was not even close to perfect... There was a thunderstorm. People started to move a little and were not as stable as before.

Adeline was glad she heard no bell noises and nothing interesting had happened yet and she hoped it wouldn't happen soon. The weather was now getting out of control.

Adeline told to Avery, 'Avery, how will we figure out who are my parents, who is the person who always speaks, and who these people are? It must sound easy, but easier said than done.'

'Oh', Avery turned as red as blood because she was so embarrassed, 'Well... I haven't thought about that you see. Well, I know we'll meet them soon so we can maybe distinguish the faces, perhaps.', Avery said in an uncertain voice.

'Well, there's something else to figure out. You remember the day I was taken away from you guys, those people took my blood and were making a potion, we need to figure out

what it is. But, as I said before, easier said than done.',
Adeline said giving a reassuring smile.

'Adeline, you know that we were expecting to find a dwarf like you. One day the dwarves' discoverers found a book and a page. On that page was written. 'Avery took a deep breath and started saying the word which she had memorized. 'On a Sunny Thursday afternoon, you'll find a girl who will save the world with all she can do. She will open this book and find a lot more. No one else than the girl will be able to open this book. I wonder what there is in the book. When we return, we'll see if the book will open. Many people tried to open it but nobody succeeded. Someone even tried to steal it.'

30

After a few hours, Felicia came rushing to Adeline with a worried face. 'Adeline Bianca's seasick and she's vomiting a lot, we have no medications, I tried to conjure them, but it didn't work. In this area, in the deep oceans, it never works. What do we do? You need to come help. By the way, Elijah and Pathfinder, did they find any sign of danger?'

'I'm coming straight away. And no, they didn't find any danger, I've been going around the ship and everything's fine don't worry about that. Let's worry about the present', Adeline said rushing behind Felicia.

In a few minutes, they arrived at where Bianca was, she was vomiting a lot and she couldn't stand up, Alden had bought a bucket for her to vomit in so it wouldn't mess up the ship.

'Felicia help me carry her to a room, there's a bed there too.' Felicia took the legs and Adeline took her by the hands. In a few seconds, they set Bianca on the bed and told her to sleep.

But Bianca wasn't good at all and she was vomiting too much to sleep.

Adeline remembered seeing a medical room so she went to search for it and remembered her directions. When she returned, she told Felicia to help her again.

They rushed there as quickly as possible. When they

arrived, they put Bianca on the bed. Alina collected all the right medications and gave it to Bianca. Bianca felt a little better and stopped vomiting but she still couldn't move. Adeline announced, '2 people leave your guns and go to the canons to take over please.'
After that Adeline made sure Bianca was better and left with the others but let Alina be there so if anything happened, she could help and she could talk to her to distract her a little.
Avery asked, 'What happened?'
'Oh, Bianca got seasick and started vomiting we put her in the medical room and gave her the medications. Alina is with her now in case anything happens. That's why I told 2 people to control the canons.', Adeline said.
Adeline was glad no one had come to attack. The weather wasn't good at all and there was a cyclone.
A few days passed and they were running out of food quickly. Water wasn't a huge problem though.
Adeline was feeling drowsy.
Elijah announced, 'I can see a sea creature which looks like a Basilisk and a Black Shuck joined together whatever you do don't look at it straight in its eyes, it's coming in our direction everyone get ready with your guns, canons, and get ready to help reload their stuff. Me and Pathfinder will take over the gun that the two people had left so they could occupy the canons.'
Adeline was just about to say it was going so well. Adeline thought this was going to be easy but it was then that she remembered she couldn't use her powers. She was now dead.
All the times she depended on her powers and she would survive but without her powers, she was as useless as a rock.

The creature started getting closer and closer and with every second Adeline felt more useless. Avery and Adeline put the canons in the direction of the creature and were ready to shoot it.

The creature was now close enough to shoot. Adeline looked at its body but didn't dare look at its eyes.

Adeline gripped her hand on the canon and started muttering the instructions that Alden had said to use the canon.

Adeline shot the creature many times but it caused no damage. The guns were running out of bullets quickly. And still, the creature wasn't dead yet, but, then Adeline thought, 'The creature doesn't have to die it just had to get away from us.'

The creature was as big as 4 humans and it wasn't that big so it wouldn't need a lot of bait to get away from the ship. Adeline went to the place where all the food was stored and bought 30 fish. She then shot it as far as she could.

The creature got attracted to it and started going towards it and by the time it was done eating the 30 fish, the ship was far away.

A whole week had passed and the weather was extremely bad. Pathfinder announced, 'The weather has been really bad and the spell now is now no longer there so we can't control the ship.'

31

Adeline woke up from her sleep by stretching her hands drowsily. She looked around and gasped she was alone on an island.

She was in a forest and she was so terrified. She heard the sound of rustling of bushes, so, she went towards the sound. She was glad to see the others there.

Adeline told everyone to follow her. They started walking and found a giant, old, and mossy wooden edifice. Adeline didn't want to step even her toe in there, but any shelter is better than in the woods. They entered it. But, as soon as they all entered the edifice the door closed and locked itself up.

Adeline froze, what were they going to do now? Her legs felt like they were noodles, too weak to move. Her mind was not able to function properly and her hands were shaking.

Adeline's skin quivered she had no idea of what to do now, where was the key?

Adeline took some time to digest her surroundings. It was dilapidated and decrepit because of how old it was.

It was a castle, it was a pretty big one, and Adeline hoped there was no one else instead of them.

Adeline decided they should explore this place. While exploring this place they might also find the key out of this behemoth-sized castle.

On the first floor, there was a giant living room that was half the size of Adeline's house in New York. It had 5 couches which were red and made out of wool to show the sign of royalty. There was a table in the middle of the couches which was made of African Blackwood and was embroidered with tiger's eyes. There was a carpet below made of wool.

However. All the beauty of the living room was destroyed because all the furniture was mottled and torn. Adeline started to climb the stairs and every step she took it would made a creak and it was noisy.

Once everyone was safely up on the next floor they started to explore again. There was a master bedroom and a kitchen. In the master bedroom, there was a bed the size of 2 Alaskan king beds joined together, on the bed were two snug pillows and a fleecy red blanket.

It seemed to be the queen's room because there was a place to apply makeup, there was a mirror and a stool in front of it.

The mirror was embroidered with pink diamonds. Adeline looked at the place enigmatically. In the makeup stand, there was a toothbrush made of wood and leaves, a plum that somehow didn't decay, and a brush made of wheat.

Looking at Adeline's confusion, Avery said, 'This, is the makeup that the people used to use in the old days in the dwarf's area, they put a spell on the makeup products so they don't decay. All the products are natural, they still work well you can try them on.'

Adeline denied she hated makeup. There was a walking closet full of old-fashioned clothes, shoes and scarves which all were old and looked very uncomfortable.

There was a shelf full of plants that were growing plenty of colorful flowers. There was a bathroom too. It was extravagant.

The 3rd floor had a kitchen and a bedroom. In the kitchen there was no electrical appliance, Adeline saw some mossy wood, and some ice which was spelled to keep cold so that they could use it as a fridge and cupboards to store everything.

In them, there was exorbitant cutlery made out of pure gold. Adeline couldn't believe how she could survive like this; it was a nightmare. The next bedroom was a little bigger than the queen's room. It seemed to be the king's room.

There was a giant bed fit for a queen or wait isn't it a king? The blankets and the pillows were made of gold and comfy. Next to the bed was a stool which on an oil lamp laid. There was a mirror with some lotion and a comb made out of branches.

There was a cupboard full of clothes, a big bookshelf, and some plants, there was also a bathroom which looked exactly like the one in the other bedroom.

On the 4th floor, there was another small bedroom. It was smaller than Adeline's room in New York and that made her surprised.

In the room there was a cupboard full of baby clothes and a door, Adeline pushed open the door to open the door and saw a crib in which a baby lay, Adeline was shocked. The baby had green skin. Adeline screeched.

32

There was no time to think as some creatures entered the room and even the baby in the crib turned into one of them joining the group.

The creatures were murderous goblins, they were pretty short with long teeth, and thin hands armed with long talons. Large red eyes, green skin black boots, pointy ears, brown ragged clothes, and a red cap with blood dripping from it.

There were 10 of them. And they looked like they didn't want to be messed with. Adeline started running as fast as she could.

'Everyone, doing any harm to this creature, called Redcap, don't let it get your blood because if we leave its cap have no blood on it will die. So, the goal is just to keep away from them and try not to drip even a drop of blood. When we are all together and when the redcaps are far away from us, we'll all make a cross with our hands to make them disappear.', Avery screamed over the sound of the terrified people shouting because they were scared out of their wits so that she could be heard.

The redcaps started to throw rocks at them. The redcaps all separated so they could corner people. Adeline was distracted, running so fast and trying to find the key to get out of the castle that she tripped on a rock that the redcap had thrown.

The redcaps started surrounding her and they got closer and closer ready to kill their prey and dip their cap in the blood. Adeline knew she couldn't escape; this was the end of her life.

Madson saw Adeline and without losing any time he took some rocks and threw them at the redcaps. The 5 redcaps turned around and looked furiously at Madson.

Adeline felt relieved she was now saved. 'Madson might be funny, but he is really brave, caring, and kind.', Adeline thought.

Now she was safe, but not the others, so, she rushed to help Madson, she saw him making a cross in front of the redcaps, they yelled and vanished behind in flames, leaving behind 5 large teeth.

Blood was dripping from Madson but he didn't seem to even notice it. But he noticed Adeline's blood oozing from her. Madson rushed to Adeline and asked, 'Are you alight, you're bleeding.'

'Yes, brother, I am. You should be asking that question to yourself. Look at you, you're bleeding way more than me! Thank you so much for saving me, how can I thank you?', Adeline said.

'By staying safe. Come on, we need to go, there are no redcaps left that's the good news but the bad news is that we can't find the key.', Madson uttered with tears in her eyes.

'Madson, why are you crying?', Adeline asked.

'It's just, we've lost so many people and one turned out to be my twin sister, it just makes me cry. And also, I'm scared that Alden and Alina will die. It's just so intense.', Madson muttered.

'Me too, but you can't be thinking of that all day, we must

move on and let go of Caliana. We have a lot in front of us and crying it all out won't help. No matter what happens I will always be there for you and you will always be there for me. We can count on each other.', Adeline said with a comforting smile.

'Yes.', Madson said pulling Adeline into a cozy hug. Adeline held tightly not wanting to face all the other problems. Madson's tears made her clothes wet.

Adeline missed Caliana too and in a few seconds, she started crying. Finally, Madson let go and they rushed to find the key.

They searched all around the castle, under the bed, in the drawers, in the pillows, in the wardrobed, in the pots, and the crib. They searched all around but nothing was found only webs.

Adeline pulled the cover and screamed at the sight of spiders crawling out towards her. She fainted.

33

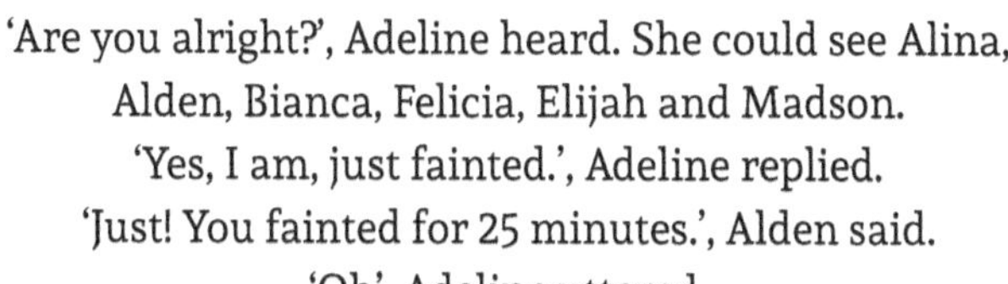

'Are you alright?', Adeline heard. She could see Alina, Alden, Bianca, Felicia, Elijah and Madson.
'Yes, I am, just fainted.', Adeline replied.
'Just! You fainted for 25 minutes.', Alden said.
'Oh', Adeline uttered.
'Well actually Dad it's 24 minutes, I counted it precisely with my watch', Madson said pointing at the watch on his wrist.
'What was the reason you fainted?', Alina asked.
'Oh, I'd rather only say it to one person.', Adeline turned as red as a tomato at that moment.
'Tell me', Alina said promptly.
Alina and Adeline went to a corner and Adeline started talking, 'When searching for the key, I looked under the covers and I saw spiders and I'm really scared of spiders, so, I think that's why I fainted, I know it's a little stupid.'
'Oh, you're just like me, I'm scared of spiders too, Madson, but not Caliana. She's not like me, only the looks, I don't know why, not even her voice, it sounds completely different from mine or Alden's. It's strange. But, one thing's for sure, Caliana cares for us but Madson not really.', Alina said.
'Mom, what are you talking about, Madson cares about you just how much Caliana does. You know what happened

just an hour ago. Madson saved me from being dead, he even put his life in danger to save mine, he was crying because of the loss of Caliana and he's scared that you guys might die too.

He might not show how much he cares about you, but he loves you a lot.', Adeline said.

'I heard my name, not once but 4 times. What are you talking about me?', Madson said peeping from somewhere and then revealing himself.

'I was talking to Adeline about how afraid you are of spiders.', Alina said with a cheeky grin.

Madson turned red and was about to go when he said, 'Oh yeah, someone found the key, I don't know their name. We opened the door.

'We have escaped the castle but not the island, these enemies are trying to kill us, we should be careful. We need to find our ship, quickly. Everyone follow me.', Adeline said. Adeline tried to use her powers but to her disappointment, it didn't work! 'My powers don't work!', Adeline exclaimed.

'We need to keep ourselves armed, all our weapons are in the ship. Who here are in their 30s or 20s, you know exactly what we're going to do!', a girl shouted out.

Adeline looked muddled and asked Alina what was happening and she said with a giant smile, 'I miss the old days but now it's finally coming back. We used to play this game before when we would be put in 2 groups. We would collect many branches and sharpen them up. Then we would make a bow each, it didn't take long though, now I'm a master at it, then we used to shoot a tree, Adeline, do you remember that tree in the back of our house there's a giant and old tree. There we used to shoot our bows at it that's why there are several marks on it. Well, it's really fun, I'll teach you how to make them, though you need to learn how to shoot or it's really dangerous, you could shoot yourself. One day when I was small, I was playing this game with my friends one of them was new to it, so I taught her how to play it but she didn't understand however, she still decided to try and shoot herself in the face, luckily my father was a doctor so he knew exactly what to do, luckily, it was fixed though today she has a giant scar on her right cheek and I feel really bad for her. Come on, I'll show you how to make them.'

Alina showed everyone how to make them and Adeline knew exactly how to make them. She collected all the materials and made her bow and arrows and even helped some other people do them.

Once they were all done, Adeline took on the lead once more and started walking deeper and deeper into the woods and found a big giant boar, it started to come towards Adeline, its only goal, was to kill people.

Adeline took her bow and shot the boar, as it was wearing a fleece that would cure it whenever it got hurt. They just had to remove that, Adeline said, 'You need to help me, some people come with me and shoot it, the others pull the fleece off of that boar. One, two, three, Go!'

With that, all of them shot the boar again and again keeping the boar distracted so that it wouldn't think of the fleece, and at the correct time, they removed the fleece on the boar and all of us shot the boar at the same time and it died.

Adeline headed farther and farther and it was a miracle when she saw their boat wasn't damaged. The other side was trying to kill them because they had sent several creatures or animals to kill them.

Adeline rushed back to the boat and her magic powers were working once more. She said to Elijah to put the boat

to sail.
After a few minutes, they were in the sea where her powers no longer worked.

34

Adeline panicked, Elijah and Pathfinder had just announced that they could see a ship a little far away. The moment she was really scared for was coming. Her heart was racing and she wanted to cry but she held in her tears. It was the time that she would die. After a few minutes, the ship was in sight, it started moving closer and closer until it stopped. Avery looked at Adeline and said, 'Now we might figure out who they are, we are not missing any chances, only if it's dangerous. They're targeting you; I don't know why. But we need to find the leader and kill her or him. That's the most important thing.'

The other ship had a name written on it and it read, 'Nickap'

And Adeline now came to realize that their ship had a name too and it was, 'Probeel'

Adeline shouted, 'reveal yourself. Coward!'

'How dare you speak to me like that!', a similar voice spoke from behind her clothes. One thing Adeline knew about the leader was that she was a girl and probably someone she knew.

The Nickaps were going to start shooting Adeline when the leader said to them with a serious tone, 'Don't shoot her, bring her to me.'

The Probeels were now alert, they had to save their master

and the others from getting hurt.
The Nickaps jumped out of their boats and landed on the Probeel. Adeline rushed to the guns and started shooting them. She turned around to see a Nickap approaching her she refilled the gun and shot him several times but nothing happened to him.
He had the golden fleece! He had stolen it from them. Adeline shouted, 'Probeels, get back the golden fleece it's with the Nickaps.'
Two Probeels came, one of them removed the fleece and the other one kept the man distracted while Adeline crept from behind and stabbed him with her sword.
Blood dripped from the man but Adeline didn't feel any pity or sorrow. Adeline rushed to the top of the ship and looked around, there was blood all over and she didn't know if it was the blood of the Nickaps or the Probeels, she hoped it was for the Nickaps.
She had come up with 5 other people. They all started shooting the Nickaps from different directions. Even though they did that there were still 3 left.
The 5 other people went down to do their jobs and Adeline was going to fly and sneak on one of the Nickaps When a cold hand grabbed her shoulder. Adeline turned around shaking with fear. A Nickap had caught her.
He grabbed her arms and pulled her to the other ship by flying. Adeline had tried to escape his grip but his hands were as tough as iron so there was no chance she could escape.
She looked at the dim light which was that maybe she could reveal the leader's identity, after all, they were going there right now. Adeline kept her sword ready. She had some sharp sticks with her too. But she didn't believe that she could fight against so many people who are adults.

She was a baby in front of them, she was not good at fighting at all. Millions of doubts were in her head but she had to focus on the present for now. In a few seconds, they reached the Nickap.

Adeline's heart beat faster than ever and her hands trembled, she felt like a noodle, she felt like she couldn't stand. However, she pushed all those things away and focused on three words. 'Fight, Survive, Repeat!'

The man took her to the leader who was waiting eagerly. 'Time to kill you, so let's make a deal, if you even touch me or my mates then I'll kill all your mates and the ones in our ship, they're already suffering waiting for someone to save them. But who knows maybe all those 70 people will get killed because of one stupid little girl. The life of at least 100 people lies in your hands. It's all up to you. And all the Nickaps don't you dare involved in this.'

Adeline and the leader moved in a circle, the leader took her sword out and aimed for Adeline little did she know, Adeline had been practicing several dodges lately and she had become good at them.

After several dodges, Bianca, Aliana, and Madson jumped to the Nickap bringing with them their swords and guns.

35

When they were by Adeline's side, she felt more confident. She took out her sword and rushed to the leader to stab her but she was good at it too.

The other Nickaps immediately joined too. They started shooting the Probeels. The other Probeels joined. The Nickaps and the Probeels started fighting and soon when the Nickaps were distracted, Adeline started to search for the other 70 people.

She went to the weapon' room and tried to open the door but it was locked.

She looked around to see any hiding places for keys when she saw a safe with a button. She pressed the button and the safe opened and inside were several keys, she searched for the smallest one as the keys in the safe were big and Adeline wondered how they even fit in the safe.

When she found the key, she inserted it in the lock but it didn't open. She took the biggest key and tried to put it inside and somehow the keyhole grew bigger until it reached the size of the key.

The door swung open and inside were several people with their legs and hands tied. Their mouths were tabbed and all of them were tied together making it harder to escape. Adeline rushed and didn't lose any time to remove the rope that had tied them all together. After that, she started to untie the people's hands only and old them to untie their legs and remove the tape from their mouths as now their hands were untied. After a few minutes, all of them were free. She told them to take the weapons there and come outside to help them. Now they were dominating the Nickaps, at least she thought that.

When Adeline was returning with the others to the fight she saw another locked door and on it was written STAFF ONLY in red. Adeline wondered what there was inside of that.

Adeline decided to fight from the other ship. She took some volunteers to the Probeel. When they reached Adeline ordered 3 other people to go to the canons and 4 people to use the guns.

'Be careful everyone, don't shoot our teammates!', Adeline shouted out to the other 7 people.

After telling what the others should do, Adeline jumped back to the nap. The leader was not being attacked right now so, she sneaked right behind her and started to pull her sword out when a Nickap came behind Adeline and was going to stab her luckily, she was aware of what was happening so she immediately turned around and stabbed him.

The leader hearing the sound that was made, turned around, now alert to her surroundings. 'Oh look who we've got here the baby girl'

'I'm not a baby'

'Oh well, then why did you cry that night in your house when Madson took away your snuggly teddy bear? You're 12 and you still sleep with teddies! That's pathetic, Adeline.'

'How do you know that!'

'I have my ways, little girl! Now don't talk your way out of this, I won't fall for that.'

After that, the leader called a Nickap to come and help.
Adeline shouted out, 'Shoot!'
From the Probeel, the people started shooting the Nickap
and the leader.
Adeline saw something strange in the leader's pocket. She
saw a key in her pocket. It was probably the key to the door
that she had passed by when she was returning to the fight.
Adeline shouted, 'Shoot the legs'
They immediately started shooting their legs and when the
leader jumped, the key fell from her pocket. Adeline threw
fire in front of the leader to make her vision blurry and
took the key before she realized it.
When they were still distracted Adeline went to find the
door.
After a few minutes, she found it, she unlocked it with the
key and pushed the door open. Inside there was a giant
cauldron that was brewing. She made sure there was
nobody in the room and went inside.
When she got in, she locked the door from inside. She
looked at the potion which was still brewing and saw that
it was a hickory colour. It didn't look too appetizing. There
was smoke all over the room. She saw several shelves in the
room which were full of glasses containing different
liquids.
Adeline wondered what the potion was for, it was not like
the one in Slopindon which makes people look way
younger than they look.

36

Adeline looked around to find some clues. After a few minutes, she found a potion recipe book, in it was the recipe for the hickory-coloured potion.

Make the Yonetheus potion

10 tablespoons of ocean water.

2 nails, cut into small pieces

8 pieces of hair.

Mix for 5 minutes and let it for 3 days

2 eyeballs

3 more nails, cut into small pieces, put it in one by one

20 flower petals (each of them must be from a different type of flower)

30 cups of clean water

2 strawberries

10 crushed blueberries

Leave for 5 days and cover it with a lid

Add another 10 tablespoons of ocean water and 10 flower petals

Cover it with a lid and after 3 years come back to it

Add 3 drops of special blood

Mix with a wooden spoon for 10 minutes

Leave for 1 day and keep it covered with a lid

Wait for the full moon and then do the main step

Summon an alicorn, if the alicorn is afraid then you will

not be able to proceed, so make sure it has extreme care.
For a few minutes, feed it with the specific food.
When it's satisfied, take off the horn without it seeing you.
Take the horn and keep it in the Prometheus potion you made in the first step. After a few minutes get the horn out, cut it into pieces, and put them into the potion, mix it for a minute and it's ready. Drink a cup of it and you will become Immortal!

'This is so cruel.', Adeline thought

Next was another recipe for a potion which Adeline thought was the Yonetheus potion and for sure it was.

3 cups of ocean water mixed with 5 cups of clean water

7 seashells

3 cups of sand

A bird's feather

1 cup of ocean water

Boil it

Let it cool down for 5 minutes and start mixing it and it's ready

This one is pretty simple, Adeline thought. She kept wondering what was the cause of these potions.

50 cups of ocean water

2 pinches of salt

7 egg yolks

3 cups of pollen

5 egg shells, crushed up

Take the yonetheus potion and keep a bone in it for a minute, after that take it out, cut it into very small pieces, and put it into the potion.

Boil it, cover it with a lid, and let it cool down

Mix for 5 minutes and now it's ready. Sprinkle it around, the effect will come after five minutes. After those five minutes, whoever comes near on o the potion will fall

asleep for 12 hours.
'Some words have been cut out from this one, but why.',
Adeline said quietly.
5 cups of clean water
3 spoons of brown sugar
1 pinch of pink salt
1 pear and apple crushed up
1 cup of milk
Mix for 5 minutes. After that, your time-traveling potion is ready, though you can only go to the past with this potion. Just drink 1 cup of the potion and then say how far back you want to go. And when you want to come back just say, back to the present.
This was a big room. After looking around the room for some time she encountered another cauldron and on it was written time travelling potion and it also looked like it was ready.
She took a cup from the shelf, then she scooped up the potion, oh it looked disgusting. But she had to discover something, and maybe this would help.
'Let's go 1 week in the past.'

37

She walked to the place where they would be fighting. The leader was still wearing her mask. Adeline was a ghost, she could pass through walls, and nobody could hear, feel, or see her.

'This is so cool', Adeline said to herself. She went closer to the leader to hear the conversation. She was talking to one of the Nickaps.

'You idiot, I sent you there for you to get the blood from Adeline, I told you a million times, 3 drops of blood. 3 drops of blood. And in case you forget, I even told you to write it in your hand. And now what do you return to me, 2 drops of her blood! You know exactly what I do when people must be punished, I like to change them sometimes though, some are more brutal than each other.' The leader shouted, smiling a cheeky smile at the end.

The leader took a rope and tied it around the Nickap then, she carried him to one of the canons. She lit the rope on fire and shot him away to the middle of the sea.

Adeline felt sorry for that guy, but again he also had the aim to kill Adeline, but deep inside her heart she felt sorry for him. The leader was very strong but she used it in the wrong way. She was the cruelest person she ever met in her whole life.

She followed the leader and listened closely to what she

told.

'Stupid Nolan doesn't remember a thing. And now what will I do, I don't have her blood. Oh, look here's an island, I'll just put the sleeping potion right here and put the spell which will lure people to the island, so when they pass, they will come here and then they will fall asleep and I'll collect her blood. This is simpler than I thought. I'll go tell the others to stop here.', the leader said smiling.

She ran to the Nickaps and told her plan. They started pouring the potion on one side of the island and then hid on the other side. After waiting for just a few minutes which felt like 10 hours to Adeline, the Probeel arrived due to a strong storm. Adeline remembered this moment they had come here and she had seen some wooden structure on the other side but she had thought it was just a tree so she didn't tell anyone about it.

She regretted that now, whatever potion that was, the Nickaps would be successful. Adeline knew she had to stop it but she couldn't do anything now she just had to see her blood being taken.

If she tried to stop the leader, she would just pass through her body, now the power was not cool.

The leader started running to Adeline. The ghost Adeline watched her succeed. But now, she had to do something. Before, when she had come to the island, all of them had gone to the old castle and when she was exploring it she had seen something weird, it was a tooth, when the redcap died it had left behind a tooth but she didn't have the time to collect it.

She rushed to the castle waiting for the time. She suffered to look at all the blood that was there.

Then the time came, she was being chased by a redcap, she started to run as fast as she could, the redcap was throwing

stones at her.
Then, she showed a cross, and the redcap screamed and left behind a tooth. The ghost Adeline, magically, was able to pick it up. She then thought that that was enough information for now.
'Wait a second, I don't remember the phrase, it's ok Adeline, you can go check the book.'
Adeline rushed to the Nickap before it would sail away. She ran to the potion book looked at the phrase and said it out loud. 'Back to the present!'

38

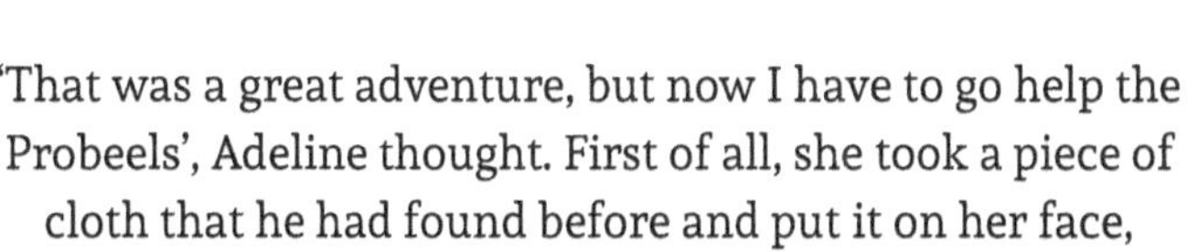

'That was a great adventure, but now I have to go help the
Probeels', Adeline thought. First of all, she took a piece of
cloth that he had found before and put it on her face,
leaving two holes in her eyes so that no one would notice
her.
She ran as fast as she could to the fighting area. She had
kept the tooth in her pocket so that no one would see it.
She checked her watch it was 1 PM and very close to
midnight, but maybe they had a chance, maybe they were
not coming to that step yet. Adeline had to stop them.
While Adeline was thinking of all these things, she didn't
realize that she was being followed. A Nickap leaped on
Adeline's back about to kill her, however, Adeline was
strong, and she pushed her shoulders behind making the
Nickap fall.
He had wet and untidy hair full of seaweed, he was
wearing wet clothes, as if he jumped straight into the sea
and came back up to the ship.
Adeline quickly took her sword. The Nickap got up before
Adeline had the chance to kill him. They started to move in
circles getting ready to attack each other.
The Nickap she was fighting was not strong at all. But he
looked similar. She thought for a couple of seconds then
she remembered, he was the one who she thought had

died, turns out, he was alive.

'It's you, Nolan. I know you, well kind of.', Adeline said.

'How do you know my name? And who are you?', Nolan said not understanding a single thing.

'Follow me, I'll explain everything, it's a long story.', Adeline said. She walked to the potion room and Nolan followed her with full trust.

When they reached, she opened the door and when they both were inside locked it up.

'So let me explain. Just one question before that, are you helping the leader of the Nickaps?', Adeline asked.

'I learned a lesson when the leader threw me in the ocean and it's to never trust her. And no, I don't help her. And you still haven't answered my questions, how can I trust you?'

'Okay, I'm Adeline.' She said, removing her mask. Nolan was surprised, 'It's you! The one that all the Nickaps are going after! I'm sorry that I tried to kill you, anyways I wouldn't be strong enough to.'

'Aren't you the one who collected all some of my blood and forgot to bring the perfect amount of blood to the leader? And because of that, you are thrown into the sea. And by the way, I know all about this because I went back in time by using a potion form here.'

'Makes sense, and yes, I am the one who came to collect your blood. And I didn't forget it, I did it on purpose, I didn't want them to prepare the potion, but they found the solution. I don't know what it is because I just came here a few hours ago. You will have to explain a lot of things to'

'Sure, I will. How did you come back to the ship after being kicked miles away from the ship on fire? That seems impossible!'

'So, the leader threw me from the canon, and I landed miles away. I decided to go to an island nearby and they soon arrived there and even stopped the ship giving me an advantage to take all my time, plus, there were no people. It was a great opportunity so I made sure that I didn't miss the boat'

'Nice one'

'Thanks, you know miss the boat, even though It wasn't a boat'

'So, it's not much of an explanation. Just that we're fighting. And who's the leader?', Adeline asked.

'Actually, I don't know. So, in the group of Nickaps, there are the trustable and the serviceable. I was one of the serviceable. Only the trustable knows the leader's identity, the leader doesn't trust the serviceable too much. They must go through several tasks to become one of the trustable. I was almost going to become one of them but, I wasn't able to let them succeed.'

'OH, I have an idea. I believe that we'll be able to stop them from doing this potion. You must become one of the trustable, then we'll know the leader. You must gain her trust. Collect my blood. Just tell her that you managed to capture me and take the extra drop of blood but then I escaped when you went to attack some other Probeels.'

'Yeah, that's good.'

'But if you wanted to stop them from making the potion, why did you even take my blood?'

'The leader threatened something. I mean she or maybe she or he is a he. I have no idea what the hell I'm saying. Oh well, let me get back to the subject. Well, so, that day she sent me to take 3 drops of your blood she told me that if I didn't go, she would have crucially killed me. So, I came to take your blood but instead of taking 3 drops I took 2 acting as if I forgot to take 3 drops.'

'I'll close my eyes, take my blood quickly, and give it to the

leader, this plan better work, it's our only hope.'
Nolan went to the shelves to take a syringe and put a sharp and long needle in it. He pulled the plunger and started pulling some blood out of Adeline. Adeline squeezed her eyes shut. She always had a fear of needles and it didn't help anymore when Nolan said that he had never used a syringe.

Finally, it was over. Adeline gasped for air; she had been holding her breath all this time because she thought that it somehow help her.

'Ok. This has to work. We can't waste any time, go ahead, find the leader, and give her the blood.', Adeline said with all the power she had left.

Adeline went back to help in the fight. When she arrived next to the fight scene, she saw the leader was doing nothing. She approached her, but there was nobody next to her. She was alone with no Nickaps to defend her.

Adeline ran towards her but when she was a few meters away 5 Nickaps came to defend the leader.

'Just when I have a chance to talk to her alone. It almost seems like I know her', Adeline said in a low voice so that no one would hear her.

Adeline started walking to the fight scene and finally arrived. The Probeels were killing several of the Nickaps and the number was becoming more even.

Adeline had said to Nolan that they would meet every night. Adeline had to stop this, she wanted to solve this mystery, who was the leader?

She had many other questions, who were her parents, why did they leave her and there was way more but not a single answer to all of those questions, there were more questions than answers. She didn't want to live her whole life like this, she wanted to figure out these mysteries as quickly as possible.

After many hours, Adeline went to the Probeel ship and waited for Nolan to come. After a few minutes, Nolan arrived with a big smile on his face.

'What happened? Tell me the whole story. I'm so excited.', Adeline almost screamed.

'Ok but no interruptions please'

'Sure.'

Nolan took a deep breath and started to tell the whole story, 'So, I went to give the leader the blood. She was happy. But like her usual self never grateful and always wants me to do more to prove I can be trusted. She said exactly this I made sure to remember every single bit of information. 'I know that you can become one of the trustable however you need to do many tasks for me and this will last for 1 more day and you will receive the trustable badge with your name on it. There are 4 tasks in all. Today you already did one which was to do an act without me telling you which will help me. Today we will do 1 more task. At night you will be able to relax. As night time is coming up soon we can't do more than 1 task. I'm just going to give you a piece of paper with all the tasks written on it so that you know what to expect.' Ugh, that took me a long time to by heart. Ok here's the paper she gave me.'

Nolan pulled out a folded piece of paper from his pocket and gave It to Adeline.

. Do an act that will help me.

. Be able to protect me.

. I need to gain your full trust

. Master shooting, sword fighting, and armless fighting so that you can fight in any condition.

39

'Today. Nolan is the most important day because you will be mastering the most important skill. Whenever we are in this step, I always bring the person with me with some other trustworthy person to a place very few people know. There, I will see if you can become one of the trustworthy, and tomorrow, I will see if you're worthy enough to get the badge with your name on it. Now first of all show me your black bracelet.', the leader said to Nolan early in the morning.

Unlike Adeline and every other dwarf in the whole world, this team of dwarves was different and they had the most powerful and most expensive ones. They were very rare to find as they were made only by one dwarf and the material was also very rare. One dwarf called, Martinald Ronsoron was doing his regular job in Tolongo (Another place like Slopindon) which was to mine, he came across something that caught His attention. Something that blended with the color of the rocks. It was also as big as a rock Martinald took the unknown stone and took it with him without telling anybody. He found it on the 3rd of August 2020. When he went back home, he went through a book which showed every single stone and gem that had been discovered until then but he didn't find any looking like the one he had found so, he got excited. He took a chest and kept it safely there by putting a padlock, casting a thousand spells on it, and then keeping it in another hiding place. The next day, when he returned to the caves, he realized that these stones were not common at all. After a few years of searching and experimenting, he realized that these stones only grew in some parts of Toronto where there was not much darkness. Where there was no rain or sunshine which made it very rare. When he was working with some of the 5 black gems he found, he decided to name the stone and called it Martiron stone.

He took the stone and started making the magical bracelets with them, after making all of them, he showed it to the public, but not many people were interested in it because they didn't know much about it. However, it did catch someone's attention and it was the leader.

She knew there must be something special with it so she went to the tiny shop where Martinald was selling gems and the special bracelet and she took all of them, Martnald was shocked that she had so much money but, he ignored that and stared at all the money he had gotten from her. When Caliana bought them, she asked Martinald about all the power it had and how to use them and Martinald gave a paper to her with everything explained on it. Martin didn't have a printer so, he had written all of it.

This is the Martian stone noldoto also known as a magical bracelet. There are many advantages to buying this despite its price. Once you see all of its abilities, you'll be shocked at how well these holdouts are. They have every single ability a regular Noldoto would have but it is also included with other abilities. Each Martian stone Noldoto has a number which is written on the bracelet. This number is really important. Your number will be written on the Noldoto when you buy it, to make it disappear you must say, 'Lotono rondo'. And when you want it to reappear just say the same thing. The bracelet has a special ability, it will also notice if the person who says 'Lotono Rondo' is the person wearing the bracelet.

Here are all the abilities and some properties it has-

. With this told to you can travel anywhere, just say the place out loud (An ability which all holdouts have with them)

. With this noldoto, you can breathe underwater whenever you are wearing it.

. This Noldoto allows you to fly even though you don't have that power.

. It's fireproof (A property which all noldotos have with them)

. This noldoto allows you to talk with others, however, there is another thing, when you talk, the bracelet will only allow you to listen to what the person is telling you from their own Martiron stone noldoto. You can add other Noldoto to be able to talk with you by pressing the white stone on the bracelet and just telling the number of the person's noldoto you want to talk with.

. The noldoto gives you other powers that some very rare people have.

I forgot the rest; you'll have to figure it out yourself. I'm pretty old, to be precise 95 years old. Have fun!

Ok, now let's get back to the present... Nolan and the leader squeezed their noldotos and they arrived in a big snowy yard. The yard was as big as 50 badminton courts. The wind swooshed across their faces; it was so cold!

The snow was so thick that it was enough to fit a whole cat inside of it. 'Oh yeah and here you go, it's a coat, it won't make you too warm. However it's better than nothing', the leader said, giving Nolan a coat.

Nolan stared, clearly looking like he was not grateful. No wonder he was like that. The coat was hot pink and had unicorns all over it, it was a coat for little girls. Luckily, Nolan was very thin.

'I just love annoying people! It's alright, right?', the leader said laughing out loud then having to cover his mouth because it was too loud.

Nolan forced a fake smile. 'Nolan, did I ever mention that to become one of the trustable, you must be honest?'

'No, why?', Nolan said looking confused.

The leader snickered behind her mask so, Nolan didn't see her. 'Well, I know this will make you feel a little less comfortable. But.. I can read minds...'

'I don't feel uncomfortable what are you talking about?', Nolan said clearly, lying.

'Well, if it becomes anything better, I don't read minds, I just can see your feeling, kinda, by looking at the color that pops up your head. Though, it doesn't just tell me how the person is feeling. Nothing in life is that easy, I have to by heart a list so that I know what the auras mean. Here you can take a look at the list. I always keep it with me, cause, I sometimes might also forget them. Let me just tell you, it's a lot, this is only one part of it.', the leader said proudly, bragging about herself and handing Nolan a piece of paper.

Nolan was shocked when he saw that this piece of paper was just one part of the things that the leader had memorized, though he also thought that she might have lied.

'Well let's start! We can't waste time, they're fighting back there and we need to rush back to help.', the leader said. And with that, they started their test and luckily, Nolan passed the test.

There was just one more thing to tick off to become one of

the trustable and it was one of the hardest ones. To gain the leader's full trust. This could take weeks days, hours, or even years or never happen.

The next day, Adeline was searching where everyone had gone because she couldn't find anyone on the Nickap's ship. She searched around and finally found that everyone had all been grouped up in a place. On one side there were the Nickaps and on one side there were the Probeels. There was a big gap in the middle and Adeline wondered what was happening. There was a big silence and no one was saying a word. Adeline pushed through the crowd of Probeels and was shocked at what she saw.

40

She was crying her eyes out. The leader was threatening to kill Nolan! 'OH, look who came right at the moment that I was about to kill your little friend here!', the leader said. Madson looked very angry and looked at Adeline, 'What the hell, Edline, you're friends with a Nickap! Betrayer!' 'Madson I can explain! I..', Adeline was about to say the whole thing but she got rudely interrupted by the leader who said, 'Well you see Madson, your smart, little, brave, and sneaky sister here had a clever plan. She lured Nolan to her side and both of them met and made a plan that they would make Nolan become one of the trustable so that they could know who I am. Well, get what Madson, your little sister here isn't smart enough to do a plan right under my nose and not make me realize it.'Nolan was crying and trying to escape but Adeline couldn't do anything because there were trustworthy all around those two. Adeline wished she could help him.

'Oh', Madson said, he had nothing else to say, he looked very guilty of what he had said before. The leader was a little far away from Adeline. She took her sword and was ready to kill Nolan. Adeline tried to stop her but she was too far and the leader stabbed Nolan. Adeline covered her face because she couldn't help looking at him die and all the blood that was oozing out of him.

'It's all my fault', Adeline said to herself. Then she saw a piece of paper and immediately took it. Nolan had thrown this paper just a few minutes before his miserable death which Adeline would always blame herself for. The paper was folded and it took a lot of time to unfold. She went to a place where nobody could see her and started to read the piece of paper. Everybody was still there so she was safe and nobody would be able to see the note.

Hi Adeline, I might be dead the time that you're reading this, and don't waste your time crying I know you're thinking that it's all your fault but it isn't. You didn't want to hurt me and you just wanted to do this so that we could help everyone and solve one of the biggest mysteries in the whole life of every existing dwarf. I'm so sorry I couldn't meet with you yesterday night and I wish I could say a proper goodbye to you but I didn't get a chance because the leader who I still didn't figure out the name of had captured me and kept me in a room alone which was locked. She had told me that she would kill me tomorrow in the morning so that everybody would see and especially you and I'm telling you again, you're not to blame. In the room I was locked in, there were pieces of paper bird feathers, and ink so I decided to write this because it would be very useful to you. I have nothing else but to hope that this goes into the right hands. I wrote all of this and I want to tell you that you were a big inspiration for me. Thing of the good things, not the bad things, and once more don't cry over this situation. Another thing, so, us dwarves don't have wills like you do, they have a special object with which you can talk to my dead self when I die. I have hidden it. I can't tell where it is in case this gets into the wrong hands. But I think you know where it is. This object that I said is a ring and once you wear it and say a special thing, no one but you will be able to use it, see it, and wear it. And I know you know the word that you have to say. The object is a necklace and I will be able to talk to you and it contains my whole history, goals, and thoughts. I decided to give it to you because I have no family members or real friends whom I can trust in my life but you. Don't tell this to anyone. We'll meet every night. I hope that you feel better now! Good luck. And don't cry!

This message just made Adeline cry even more as she knew exactly what word Nolan was talking about and also the place. Adeline folded the pocket and kept it safely in her pocket rushed back to the crowd and acted as if she was there the whole time. Everyone was just silent when the leader broke the silence by saying, 'Adeline what about we have a small talk. Alone, not even by guards. No fighting just a little talk.'

Madson, Alden, and Alina were shouting at me to not go, but this was a great opportunity. 'Well, well we finally get to talk alone. You really wanted to know who I am and I believe you still do so why not just get your answer it's not like it will help you beat me or anything and I'll tell you everything. Be ready to cry once more or be extremely angry or shocked. So in the beginning when I realized that you exist and you have a lot of powers I liked you and I thought that you would join the team but you didn't and I'm telling you, you'll regret it. So, tell me, do you want to know?", the leader asked.

Adeline nodded and the leader continued, 'So, well.......I won't tell you my name but let's see if you recognize me!'

The leader then removed her mask but Adeline didn't

recognize her. Then she made a bottled potion appear and drank some of it, enchanted something and then she started to change and when that was all done, Adeline was shocked at what she saw that she could almost faint, 'Ca-Caliana? I thought you were missing or dead. You're a betrayer!', Adeline shouted and stomped away to tell the news to the others. She first of all searched for Madson, Alina, and Alden because they were Caliana's family. Finally, she found them and saw that they were really angry.

'I know that you guys are angry but she did nothing to me, I know who the leader is. Be ready to cry.'

'Who is it?', all of them said in unison.

'Ca-Caliana.', Adeline said in a low voice.

'It can't be her, she's too young and she went missing recently!', Madson said and the other two. 'I saw her face and it's her. I always used to think that the announcements in the maze were similar to a voice I know and it was Caliana's all the time and we didn't even notice. When she was small and born, I don't think she was born then, I think she came in the form of a baby and acted as if she was Madson's twin, though really, she was older. I think she came there to collect some information. She has many different bodies that she can transform into, the one she is in right now is Caliana. She uses the potion every time.", Adeline said, she knew how sad they would feel.

'Show us! We need to see, just thinking that she did all of this is so weird.', Alden said.

'Sure, follow me but don't be seen by her and her guards, right now she's probably alone. Come quick she's very near.', Adeline said.

After a few minutes of crawling around, they finally saw that Caliana was no longer wearing her mask and was talking to one of the Nickaps. As soon as they witnessed that Caliana was the leader, they scooted away to a safe place.

'Oh my god, we're going to give revenge. All this time she was tight under our nose in our house and we didn't notice!', Madson said.

'Sometimes, we did feel suspicious because every time I used to clean the house early in the morning, I used to see muddy footprints and Caliana's shoes looked like they were used. These prints were not there before we all slept. Which meant only one thing, Caliana used to go out when we were sleeping at night. I told this to Alden and he said that Caliana had several friends and liked to go out with them alone so maybe that's what she's doing. So, we didn't ask any questions because some people did go out at night. But today, we know the reason.', Alina said looking very sad.

41

Adeline was back in the Probeel ship medication room where Nolan and her would always meet at the need of each day at night. Adeline wished that Nolan would appear but he didn't and she started to cry. She kept the letter that Nolan had written tightly in her hands. She had read it every single time she was free and it made her cry even more.

'Adeline, find the necklace and you'll be able to talk to him! Search!' She looked around and then remembered what Nolan had once said, 'If I were to hide any object I would have hidden it in the soil of a pot where you would grow a plant.'

She took the pot where they had planted a medicinal plant. She unrooted the plant removed all the soil from it and put it on a desk and finally found the necklace. She felt like Nolan was back alive as soon as she touched it. As soon as she touched it, warmth filled her body.

Nolan used to always say, 'Gollygoodness' which he said meant oh my goodness. Adeline hoped that this was it and said in a low voice, 'Gollygoodness' Soon the bracelet disappeared and reappeared. Soon Nolan appeared right in front of Adeline, she covered her ice and smiled with tears of joy.

'I'm so proud that you figured this out, Adeline. Well, when you get this necklace there are some things you need to know. As soon as you say anything related to this, you will forget all about the object which is called the 'Lawcot' and you will not remember a single thing about me even though people try to make you remember me. Whenever you want to talk to me you must say the word, 'lious', it's a word I created that sounds as if you're speaking gibberish when you say it and people won't notice you. Well, they won't hear you when you're talking to me because when you're talking with me time freezes only for you. The lious Is only given to your parents or someone very close.'

'But I'm not close to you.'

'You are the best person I've ever met Adeline. Okay, let me continue about the Lious. It's not something easy to handle. Every day I will tell you something, even though you don't want to, the necklace will make you feel like you want to tell it to someone. And if you do tell someone about it, let's just say you don't want to do that.'

'I don't get why Caliana would kill you, in front of the crowd, she had a mask and had said the purpose of killing you was because you knew who you were but then just a few minutes after that she relieved herself.'

'It's Caliana, like your "sister". Oh my god, that was unexpected!'

'First of all, she's not my sister, and second of all, even though she was my sister, I wouldn't care. By the way, don't take that to be offensive. Sometimes, I just say things that I don't mean and it's a problem I need to fix. So Nolan, are you sure that nobody can see the necklace whenever I talk to you and are you sure that time freezes when I talk to you?'

'Yes, I can't see the necklace myself. There's a catch, when a dangerous thing is happening, you can't talk to me and because of that, you won't be able to freeze time. Time for the first secret to tell you. Try your best not to tell anyone about it. As if your life depends on it.

'When I was smaller, like about 5 years old, I was so dumb. Caliana who then was in another body came into my house when I was all alone. She looked like a kind teenager. She gave me 2 mysterious candies and told me to give them to my parents and not eat them myself. So, after a few hours, my parents arrived, I told them that I had bought them in a shop and gave it to them. That candy was not regular. Nothing happened when my parents ate it and they told me that it was pretty tasty. But the next day, they got several health issues which could only be caused because of that candy as my parents were so healthy before eating the candy. Soon they died. I know that it's my fault and I will always feel terrible because of that. I know how you feel when you think that I'm dead because of you. If it was your fault, it wouldn't be bad. But, Ellora, don't waste your time thinking about that the next time if we talk once more, I'll tell you the next part of the story. Bye, I have to go, it's important.

Adeline wondered what he had to do which was so important. Adeline had read this letter so many times that she almost knew it by heart. Adeline decided that she would talk to Nolan at the same time and place where they used to meet before at the end of each day of his tests. Adeline thought of how Caliana had been to Nolan and all the others and felt like stabbing her.

It was the next day; it had been a long time since anyone had slept but Adeline felt like Caliana slept every night because she would never see her at night and in the morning, she looked so fresh. In the early morning, it's usually very peaceful and most Probeels go to their ship.

Adeline was walking around and suddenly stopped and hid behind a wall because she had seen Caliana talking to one of the Trustables.
Caliana was very excited and happy about what she was talking about and that made Adeline feel very scared and worried.

42

'Where am I? How did we get here?', Adeline said looking around, it was nighttime, the full moon was shining brightly. That only made Adeline remember one thing, 'werewolves. She shivered from both fear and cold. It was very cold and it was snowing! The snow sank in the water and dissolved making a shine in the water wherever it dissolved.

That was paranormal. There were several other Probeels but they were all asleep. They were in a room which was locked and they were tied to each other by a rope.

There was a glass rooftop that allowed them to see a little bit of the sky but it was slowly being covered by humps of snow. There was a key that was on the edge of a pretty tall bookshelf. They had to get that key to get out of here. Just a minute after Adeline had woken up, everyone else woke up. After adjusting to their surroundings and understanding what was happening, they started their plan. Luckily, Madson always had a pocket knife with him. He immediately cut the ropes which were tied on his hands and legs and after that, their rope was cut in half and everyone could get out of the rope.

They finally got the key. Before unlocking the door and facing all the adventures ahead of them, Adeline had something to say, 'You guys might be wondering why I haven't been around much during the night. I'm very sorry but I was trying to figure out some things. One day, I went to the potion room and found some recipes and one was for immortality. It was written that the last step could only be done at midnight during a full moon day which only means one thing. We can't let them become immortal, they'll become unstoppable causing more deaths and chaos. We need to stop them from doing the last step. Anyone has a plan. Everyone, get together and speak quietly so that the Nickaps can't hear us.'

'I do. So, everyone else except me and Adeline, try to fight off all the monsters from the cauldron, I see from the window that there's one big one with a potion brewing in it. Adeline and I will run up to that cauldron and add a few extra ingredients which will mess the potion up. It's not too solid. But let's just wing it. We can do this!'

And with that, all of them stormed out of the room. They couldn't use any of their powers and that would make this very hard.

'Everyone, watch out for werewolves. I remember studying about them. You can kill a werewolf just like you would kill a human being. The hard part is figuring out how to kill it before it will do the same to you.', one of the Probeels said.

Adeline and Madson stayed in place while everyone else stormed toward the monsters and Nickaps.

'Adeline, when my parents decided to take of you, they made me promise that I would do my best to protect you. We must stay together!'

'Yeah, yeah! We have lives to say, Madson, when will you ever get to say that in your life? I wish we had thicker coats. It is pretty cold out here. Come on now we need to go now. We can't let anyone down.'

They started to run to the cauldron while the snow poured

down. Adeline and Madson's skin shivered out of both cold and fear. Mostly fear.

They approached the higher deck and started thinking of what to do. They decided they would swing down on the electric cable and then land right next to the cauldron however it was pretty risky because they could fall right into the potion and it was boiling that they would burn to crisps and die. Was this a risk they were willing to take to save the world from these evil people? It was. It was a crazy idea of Madson which he had come up with.

'Let us just swing of the electric cable this is too high and we'll probably die.', Madson had said sarcastically. Surprisingly Adeline agreed. Madson was truly befuddled and didn't believe Adenine for a second.

They had no other choice because they had led themselves to a place where each direction they would go they would be seen by an army of Nickaps and they couldn't get caught.

The cauldron was surrounded by another army of Nickaps which they would land right next to. Adeline had to let the others know that she and Madson needed help to cross the cauldron and fight off the other people surrounding it.

Luckily before they had escaped the room, Adeline said to all of them to stay next to the cauldron until they knew that Madson and her were safe alone.

The cauldron was in a really weird place as it was found right next to the ocean. Caliana, the one who had revealed that she was the leader and they had thought was Madson's sister was right next to the cauldron expecting Adeline to come up and show herself soon enough.

So how exactly do we swing off this electric cable? That was the only question. Well, it was broken and they could just swing off but she was afraid of one thing. 'What if we got an electric shock?', Adeline asked Madson.

Madson covered his mouth so as not to make noise and reveal themselves. 'WHAT'S FUNNY?', Adeline asked in an angry but low tone.

'Adeline you know for sure that these electric cables only are for the human world. These things don't work in the dwarf world. Why would electricity work and our powers wouldn't? Anything that dwarves possess or make is way stronger than what humans make. If electricity was working here then our powers would surely work too.'

'So we just hold on to the cable and push ourselves forward and hope to land next to the cauldron and not right into the potion.' Adeline said with a scared voice.

'Yeah that's pretty much it. For once I am seeing you scared.'

'Shut up Madson your face is so small you're scared too you're just not showing it'

'No I am not scared', Madson said trying to act brave.

'Ugh, whatever. Are you ready?', Adeline asked.

'Whoa, whoa! I thought you were just kidding, I was joking. I didn't expect you to take it seriously. It is pretty risky.'

'We don't have time and I'm ready to take the risk. Madson, are you ready now? We'll go together. You below me.'

And with that, they pulled the cable towards them and carefully placed themselves.

Then, once placed they had to get out of their comfort zones and had to swing.

Madson carefully walked to the edge and then pushed his legs against the edge and they left sorting towards the cauldron. Once they were right above the spot where they wanted to land they both jumped off tumbling on top of each other.

They sorted themselves out and then they saw the other Probeels approaching ready to help them fight off the Nickaps and Caliana.

'Oh look who's here. Starting to come in time now are you Adeline? Developing a new habit? Well, you are just in time because the potion is almost ready. We have all been waiting for you.'

Adeline didn't answer and said nothing keeping her mouth shut and balling her fist. She then darted towards Caliana. Her two bodyguards blocked Adeline from even making a scratch on Caliana.

'Oh, so you wanna fight with me? Well, let's see if you'll return home safely!'

Adeline's blood boiled. She couldn't t let Caliana become immortal. She had to do something. The cauldron was covered with a thick fabric, preventing her from adding something to the potion and messing it up. What could she do?

There was no other time to think because now Caliana was not going to let her leave.

Surprisingly, nobody approached her and Caliana stood there smiling eye to eye. She had a trick up her sleeve.

But Adeline had no idea what it was and she was racking her brain for it. Then it struck.

It was the full moon and it reminded her of one thing. Werewolves! A Nickap looked up at the moon and his eyes opened wide. He did strange movements and then started transforming into a werewolf. The fur appeared all over his body and then he howled. The color of his fur was a crimson color and Adeline's body shook with fear probably the hundredth time she had been on this ship.

Usually, the werewolf would not know who to attack but Caliana had put a spell that made the werewolf target only the people she would soon say.
Her smile soon became an evil green and she told out the names of some of the Probeels and especially mentioned the werewolf to chase Adeline specifically.
In the blink of an eye, the werewolf had it's snarling face right in front of her. His teeth were so sharp and saliva dripped from them and fell on her shoulder.
Adeline would be disgusted by now and we'd rush somewhere to change her clothes but in this scenario, you would think she would run away as fast as she could.
Well, she didn't because she just stood there frozen and not a single muscle moved, she didn't even breathe. She was as stiff as a log and she just stood there. She wanted to move but her legs just wouldn't let her move at all.
Well, she stood no chance to escape without getting hurt.

43

Suddenly, Biana came and pulled Adeline away. Adeline felt so relieved that Biana had pulled her from the werewolf because then she would be infected too. Adeline ran towards the place where Adeline would usually store her swords as not many people went there, the bedroom, nobody had the time to sleep.

Time was ticking and Adeline had to move fast, the potion could be ready anytime and she had to stop it. She ran towards the bedroom as fast as she could and when she finally arrived there she easily identified the sword which was partially made of silver at the blade. Adeline had kept ready and had taken this silver sword in case of this exact scenario and it was worth it.

Adeline put her hand in her pocket and felt the cold metal which was what Nolan had saved for Adeline after his pitiful death. This made Adeline's blood boil. She needed revenge and this encouraged Adeline a whole lot. She looked around, no sign of a werewolf here, she had some rest time for now. Well, at least that's what she thought. The next second the werewolf arrived from behind the other side of the room.

Adeline was so afraid but this time she didn't freeze when the werewolf arrived a little far away from her, she lunged towards it and slashed her sword through. The werewolf cried in agonizing pain and collapsed on the floor. Red blood seeped through the cut that Adeline had made.

Caliana probably wouldn't know that the werewolf had been killed. She looked around and saw nobody. She had an idea but it was not a smart idea. She ran towards the cauldron and tried to not make her be spotted. A little far away was the cauldron she had an idea, all of the people were looking ahead so she sneaked up from behind keeping her sword ready.

Then she tried her best and used all her energy to push the cauldron toward the water so that it would just fall in the water but she couldn't. Then it struck, she wrapped her hands around the cauldron, and even though it was very hot she ignored it and then brought the cauldron with her in the water.

Soon she was falling into the water with her arms still wrapped around the cauldron. She decided to let go of it and then covered her mouth just in case she drank the potion by mistake, she didn't want to live forever, not at all! Soon she found herself in the water and she put both of her hands on her mouth and covered her eyes as they burnt.

When Adeline had pushed the cauldron down, the Nickaps had noticed and Caliana came to look at what had happened and saw that Adeline was far below the water and she thought that she was dead because she just stayed there.

Caliana smiled. "Everyone head to the cauldron, we have an announcement we would think you would like to know!" she said through an object that was functionally similar to the human mike.

Knowing something wrong was happening, when Madson arrived at the place where the caldron used to be, he saw that it wasn't there anymore, he thought of all the possibilities that there could be and what was the most logical option that could have happened.

She looked around and it was not on the ship, the Nickaps couldn't have moved it so far, and Madson couldn't see anything strange or suspicious. He thought in his mind, 'If the Nickaps couldn't make it too far and it's not around anywhere then it's not on the ship so where else could it be?'

"Well, well, well wasn't Adeline all off you people's idol, well she isn't good at all, really has a tiny, not a creative person as I see. Well, this little brain of hers made her jump into the water and she has now drowned or died 'cause I don't see anybody in the water."

In the meantime, while when all of that was happening Adelin was in the water, and she was almost out of breath, she was trying to hold her breath because she had learned it in school and if she didn't then she would have to go up and Caliana and the other Nickaps would most likely come to harm her as she was unarmed. She moved her legs and hands around. And wanted so badly to go back up to the surface.

She opened her eyes in the water and was terrified by what she saw, it was a shark approaching her. It was so giant. Adeline was so scared because she was unarmed, she had to use her strength. She remembered what she had learnt one day when she was looking at some video on YouTube.

First of all, she keeps her eyes locked on the shark so that she won't be attacked by surprise. Here yes were burning but she tried her best to keep them open for the whole time and tried to blink as little as possible. She wouldn't be able to swim to the entrance of the ship as it would be too far and the shark would easily outrun her, first of all, Adeline couldn't swim that fast, and second of all the shark would outrun anyone.

Adeline stayed as still as possible and stopped thrashing her arms and legs around as soon as she saw the shark. She remained calm. The shark was a few meters away from her so she went to the surface of the water for some air and plopped down back in the water as soon as possible keeping her eyes still on the shark.

The shark was now very close so Adeline balled her fists and aimed for the gills of the shark. It was hard as the skin was very tough. Unfortunately, this shark was not like others and immediately reacted by moving its body. Adeline tried with her legs and then gave up; it was too hard.

She had failed miserably, the shark got closer and bit Adeline's shoulder, she covered her mouth and screamed out of pain, but nothing came out as she was in the water. "This couldn't possibly be a normal shark, I know I've not experienced a shark bite, but it wouldn't hurt this bad right and it just feels different.", she thought to herself.

Then she remembered, one day, Adeline had borrowed one of Caliana's books and in it, she had read about a shark that is immortal and venomous. They're immortal because they just turn themselves into babies once they die almost just like a jellyfish.

These sharks are specifically only found in the ocean surrounding Palnoma dwarf island which was the furthest one from Slopindon. Adeline wondered how they would get back home and how many more creatures were out there. But for now, all she could think of was the terrible pain she was feeling, she couldn't describe it.

She needed to call for help, so she started blowing bubbles with her mouth. She was hopeless.

Madson was shocked by what he heard, he was so angry and fell to his knees crying, he had lost her! Then he looked into the water and saw some bubbles forming in the distance.

"Maybe there's a chance of me saving her, I can't let her die. I need to try. You can do this, Madson", he said to himself in his mind. Then he dived into the water. He swam as fast as he could and then he finally caught sight of Adeline hopeless.

He saw the blood dripping from her shoulder, what had caused this? There were several dangerous creatures in the ocean so that's why, Madson had brought a spear with him.

She decided to bring back Adeline to the hospital as fast as possible and then he looked up and saw Biana, he called her and said, 'Biana, Adeline got bitten get the bandages at the entrances of the ship, there might be some venom just bring everything we'll need."

Then Madson swam and brought Adeline to the ship entrance where Biana was waiting, fortunately, it was on the other side of where everyone was.

44

Adeline opened her eyes, she was now in the bed of the hospital in the probeel's ship. Why was she here? Then she remembered everything but how did she get here? Several familiar faces were looking at her.

'She's awake', someone said. Alden and Alina came and hugged Adeline tightly and she smiled. 'We're so glad you woke up', Alden said. 'Yeah, it's been a few hours', Alina said.

'Who saved me?', Adeline asked and Madson and Biana said, 'We did!'

Adeline hugged all her friends and family and pulled them in a tight hug. 'We're not too far from the Nickaps ship. We're leaving soon.', Elijah said.

'Wait no, no! You can't do that, we'll have to go through the maze all over again, and that can't happen, we'll lose too many people, when I had sneaked up on them from behind the cauldron, I heard them say something. They had said that they had so many teleporters in the hospital, we should go and get one, only 2 or 3 people should go. I'll go!', Adeline said.

'No Adeline, you can't, that is a severe injury you got and you can't risk anything, you must rest, Alden, Alina, and I will go.', Madson said.

And then they left.

The three of them jumped from the Probeel ship to the Nickap ship as they were so close to each other, then they went the long way to the hospital as the shortcut would be blocked by the angry Nickaps.

When they reached the hospital, they took as many teleporters as they could carry and went back to the hospital found in the Probeel ship. They all separated into 10 groups as there were 10 teleporters. Then each group stood in a circle and held onto the necklace which turned out to be the teleporter and they said, "Slopindon".

In a few seconds, they all came to the capital of Slopindon, it was as busy as usual but all of the people were tense. When they saw all of the people arrived they were shocked as in the news, these missing people were always occurring.

The news spread like fire and everybody was happy and knew what happened. Everyone that was in the maze was called to an interrogation. Madson, Adeline, Alden, and Alina headed back home happily and changed their clothes as quickly as possible, they each had a nice bath and had their breakfast.

'Well that was a terrifying experience, I'm very proud of you Adeline and Madson!', Alden said.

'Yeah, you survived!', Alina said and all of them went into a tight hug.

Part - 2

"Madson! Madson! Come down!", Adeline screamed from downstairs. It had almost been a whole year since Adeline had saved the day on the Nickap's ship and she had grown and learnt a lot more about Slopindon, she had done a lot of training and had discovered the amazing beauty of Slopindon. She had gotten used to the environment, her friends, family and school. It had all become usual.

Though when Madson, her brother, Alden and Allina, her two guardians had realised that Caliana who they thought was their family member was actually the one leading the Nickaps ready to kill them and rule the world by becoming immortal, they went through an emotional rollercoaster and the house was dull for a few weeks after the incident.

She had discovered that in Slopindon there was this gadget very similar to the mobile phone in the human world called Vallen and since she had bought one, she was able to connect with her friends and also made her feel more comfortable.

'Why? I'm in the middle of a conversation with my friend. I'm almost done talking just tell me why?', Madson shouted from his room.

'Just come down!', Adeline shouted.

'About 4 minutes.', Madson shouted back.

Soon Madson came down. 'You know you were better before, the shy girl who would never ask anyone to do anything for her.', Madson joked, that's one thing he loved, making jokes, it was almost like a family thing.

'I need help with my history homework, I have no idea who the hell Martin Criston is and I have to write a 10 pages essay about him due on Monday! Luckily, it's a Saturday and you're here!', Adeline said, grinning.

'Couldn't you have asked mom or dad, they know more than me!', Madson said clearly agitated.

'I have many reasons, it's a public holiday and mom and dad need to rest, it must be hard for them to raise a child like you Madson. Have you ever thought of that, I feel very bad for them.' Adeline said cheekily.

'You shut up!', Madson laughed.

'And you're amazing at history aren't you, or am I mistaken?', Adeline asked.

'Oh, you're right for once. I'm great at history, though I don't loove it.', Madson said smiling eye to eye.

'Guess the last reason, let's see if you remember.', Adeline said frowning making her eyebrows almost meet.

'Honestly, I have no idea. What is it? Tell me.', Madson said with no interest.

'Well, you're not a good brother at all are you. Silly! What a bad memory, tomorrow is the 16th, did you ever wonder why mom and dad had taken a holiday for tomorrow?', Adeline asked.

'What special event is there tomorrow. It's just a regular Sunday, they probably just decided to take a break because they're tired of working.', Madson said.

'No, you're terrible! Tommorow is my birthday, you nincompoop! Do you even know how old I'm gonna become?', Adeline said angrily.

'Oh, shoot, I forgot, though I do remember how old you are gonna become, 12.', Madson said with a smile. Madson was acting all this time, he knew that it was her sister's birthday tomorrow, why would he ever forget that, Alden and Allina had decided to give a surprise to her so they were acting like they didn't know it was her birthday so that it would have a better impact.

'At least come help me now, for sure you have a book or something about this guy, right?', Adeline asked.

'What's his name again?', Madson asked.

'Martin Criston', Adeline said.

'Come on upstairs, you'll help me search if there are any books.', Madson said.

And with that both of them went upstairs and started searching all the shelves for a book about Martin Criston.

'Hey, I found this book about some historical people, there might be whoever you're looking for in there, come in my room.', Madson said.

Adeline went to his room, took the book he was holding in his hand and searched through the Table of Contents and landed on the name Martin Luke Criston.

'Madson, he's in here! I found him.', Adeline said.

Madson stopped searching and sat on the bed besides her. Adeline flipped through the pages and reached the correct page.

'Well, I don't think you can turn two pages of information into a 10 page essay, just search up Martin Luke Criston on your Vallen.', Madson said after looking at the book.

'There's an app you can download that you can search for information like that?', Adeline asked surprised.

'Not only that, you can search the meaning of a word and about historical people which are famous, though you can only search for some people, there's a list of people in the description. The name of the app Histhal. It was really

useful for me. You have your Vallen on you.'
Adeline nodded.
'Give it to me, I'll install it and give you all the information about this Martin Criston.'
After a few minutes Madson had a whole pdf of 30 pages of information just about Martin Criston downloaded on Adeline's Vallen.
'Thank you so much.', Adeline said and was heading downstairs when Madson said, 'If you want anything, tell me, just don't disturb mom and dad in their rooms, let them rest. I'll cook if you're hungry, just tell me. I'm coming down too. You know what, let's have a small treat, want some Marshaps?', Madson asked.
'You know how to make them, aren't they like really hard to make?', Adeline asked.
Marshaps was one of the best snacks made in Slopindon it was small fluffy balls which when you put into your mouth would melt and burst and it would feel like you're having a party in your mouth.
'Of course I can't make them, out of all the thing I can't make marshaps, they are one thing I just can't make. Mom bought some yesterday. They're in the kitchen, come on let's have some fun.', Madson said in a tone of excitement
Adeline went straight to the kitchen and opened the drawer where Allina would usually keep all the snacks and was about to tear apart the pack of marshaps when suddenly Madson grabbed Adeline's hand.
'Not so fast little girl, first you got to do your homework! Chop!Chop! Get to work. It's just copying.' Madson said cheekily.
Adeline frowned and straight away set to work.

www.ingramcontent.com/pod-product-compliance
Lightning Source LLC
Chambersburg PA
CBHW021535150726
47990CB00006B/2248